THE GIRLS THEY FEAR

J.H LEIGH

KIMBERLY SHEETZ

To all the girls who've fought a seemingly impossible battle against foes no one can comprehend...this is for you. A bad-ass isn't someone with an absence of fear, but the grit to forge ahead no matter the obstacle. Find your inner bad-ass!

CONTENTS

COPYRIGHT

THEY GIRLS THEY FEAR

By J.H Leigh

Cover design by Richer Designs

The following **NOVEL** is approximately 51,000 words original fiction.

NEWSLETTER SIGN UP

Want to stay updated on future releases from J.H. Leigh? Of course you do! Here you go, just click the link and follow the instructions. Thank you!

CLICK ME TO SIGN UP!

A NOTE FROM JH

Dear Reader,

The saga comes to a close. I am so overwhelmed by the incredible response this series has created with readers. I am humbled and overjoyed you have chosen to go on this ride with me.

This series wasn't easy to write but it was so important to tell. Human trafficking is a major problem in today's world and there's no excuse for it. The more light we can shed on this horrific situation, the less predators can hide in the shadows.

All my love,

J.H. Leigh

1

"Don't get tangled up with Badger, he's bad news," Dylan warned with a dark scowl after I'd clicked off. "Trust me. He's like cancer. He'll eat you up until there's nothing good left in you."

"I can take care of myself. Besides, we need the money, right?" I asked, slinging my backpack over my shoulder. "I'm supposed to meet him in the back room at the club. Any tips?"

"Yeah, don't fucking go," Dylan answered. "What the fuck is wrong with you? Ever since we left the auction house, you've been different. It's like someone plucked the sense right out of your head. You're the sane one, remember? I'm the irrational fuck-up. Let's keep it that way."

I shrugged, saying, "I call it an improvement,"

She was right. I did feel different because I was different. Facing the auction house, reveling in its burnt husk, knowing I'd brought it down, poured steel courage down my spine. I wasn't afraid anymore. My fingers found the tiny cross hanging from my neck. "If you want to come along and give me some pointers, that'd be great. Otherwise, cover for me with Hicks."

"That's a turn of events, *me* lying for *you*. I don't like it."

"Life sucks. You coming?"

"You're a dick. Of course, I'm coming. If I don't go, you'll end up getting killed. The streets are rough, especially where Badger runs his business." She slung her backpack over her shoulder, resigned but still pissed. "You owe me."

"You're coming on your own. Don't slow me down." Then, we climbed out of the fire escape. Hicks was passed out on the couch from the bottle of Jack he'd started slugging back around three that afternoon. Likely, he was out until tomorrow morning, which worked perfectly.

Badger said the job would only take a few hours. With a little luck, we'd be done and back before Hicks noticed we were gone.

But even if we weren't, Hicks wasn't our dad, and he really didn't try to be, *thank god.*

That was the benefit of staying with a disgraced ex-cop turned private detective with demons he couldn't quite slay — he had no room to judge. Kerri was the one who would try to put her foot down, but she wasn't here, so I didn't have to worry about her.

We stepped into the night, wearing our wigs and hoodies, careful to avoid any CCTV and melting into the shadows. We'd become experts at hiding our faces and avoiding eye contact with anyone.

The thing was, most people didn't want to notice us. We took advantage of people's discomfort to disappear.

We were the throwaway kids, the ones that society had failed, the ones that Madame Moirai had considered easy pickings.

Maybe at one time, we had been.

Not anymore.

Kerri was chasing down leads on the mortuary that'd handled Nova's burial. Hicks was researching the title ownership of the auction house in Esterdell, trying to nail down who actually represented Avalon Incorporated. That left Dylan and me pretty much twiddling our thumbs and playing way too much solitaire.

I couldn't handle that much downtime. Not anymore.

Badger was dangerous as fuck and unpredictable, but I looked forward to the change of pace. I needed the adrenaline to power my blood to keep me going. At night I dreamed of finding Madame Moirai and stabbing a knife through her black heart, but because we didn't know who she was, the person in my dream was a faceless phantom that kept drifting out of reach.

I always woke angry and frustrated.

That was my current frame of mind — driven and full of rage.

Seemed appropriate, given our circumstances.

I turned my grief into something more useful; my fear into fuel.

And Badger, for all his many faults, served a purpose.

If I was running for Badger, I'd have a certain level of protection throughout the city, in the underground, and being a part of the shadows enabled me to listen without being seen.

It didn't matter to me that what I was doing was illegal.

That ship had sailed a long time ago.

All that mattered now? Vengeance.

And nothing would get in my way.

As crazy as it seemed, Badger owned a seedy night club and stayed in the apartment above. Until Madame Moirai had sent trained assassins to murder us in the middle of the night, we'd been staying there, too.

We killed the fuckers, but we didn't get out of that night unscathed. They killed Jilly that night. We left the scene awash in blood and gore, leaving Jilly's body behind because we hadn't had a choice. Badger handled the details.

I didn't know where Jilly ended up. I hadn't had the balls to ask.

We fell into step with each other, bound up in our thoughts as we wound our way through the crowds like shadows armed to the teeth. It felt good to be on the move. I couldn't stand to stay still anymore.

I didn't recognize myself anymore. I wasn't the naive street kid Madame Moirai had targeted, and I wasn't the girl so desperate for a second chance at life that I'd bite at the first thing dangled in front of me.

I was a predator now.

I didn't flinch at blood. I didn't blink at the thought of killing someone.

I guess it was true what they say about pushing someone past the breaking point – once you lose that essential component that walks side by side with compassion, you don't feel much of anything.

Vengeance kept me going. Maybe even some twisted form of grief as I mourned for myself and the girls we'd lost.

I hadn't known Tana or Jilly long, but somehow they'd burrowed into my soul, latched on with sharp fingers, and they were as much a part of myself as the arms and legs attached to my body.

I missed her oddly sunny optimism and the way she kept me guessing whether or not she was going to go rogue in the middle of the night.

Jilly was the only person I'd ever known who could chirp about something horrific from her past and then smile as if it'd happened to someone else.

That detachment was the hallmark of a sociopath, but there was something disarming about Jilly; it was hard to imagine her being a monster.

But I guess we were all monsters now, through no fault of our own, but the justice system wouldn't see a difference.

It wouldn't matter that we were chased until we had to fight back. People were dead. People in suits would demand their due.

Except who was demanding justice for us? For the girls who were plucked like ripe peaches and then squashed and discarded? How many girls had Madame Moirai destroyed for her little operation?

And who the fuck was Madame Moirai? How did she have access to all the broken birds in the system?

I hated mysteries before all this happened; now, I detested the lack of information that kept us in the dark.

"If your thoughts were any louder, I'd say all of New York could hear you," Dylan muttered.

Sometimes silence spoke volumes. I acknowledged Dylan with a grunt and kept moving.

We slipped down into the subway system and disappeared into the abandoned tunnels to climb into the hidden entrance of Badger's club.

The subway system was a catacomb of past, present, and future that most New Yorkers knew nothing about.

Abandoned tunnels, a thriving underground of runaways, thieves, and criminals, and one man who ruled his kingdom with an iron fist beneath the noses of normal society — it was an alternate reality that operated with its own set of rules and its own variation of justice.

Also, it was dangerous as fuck for anyone without Badger's special protection or permission to roam.

Since discovering Nova was dead, Badger was more lethal than ever. Like me, he lived on the promise of vengeance, which worked in our favor because we shared symbiotic goals.

He wanted Madame Moirai's head on a platter, and he didn't care how it happened. Her death wouldn't bring Nova back, but it might provide closure.

But who really knew? Maybe we'd kill everyone associated with The Avalon's operation, but that cold, hard knot inside our souls would remain.

It was worth a shot, though.

We found Badger in his office, looking rough as if he hadn't slept in days, but his eyes remained sharp as ever. Clenching a cigarette between his lips, he tossed a manilla envelope my way. I caught it easily. "What's this?"

"The job," he answered, inhaling and blowing out a quick plume of smoke, removing a bit of tobacco from his lip. "I need this delivered by midnight. I'll text the address to your burner. Don't let anyone get in your way. No excuses." He looked to Dylan, his gaze narrowing. "It's a one-man job. You can stay here."

"Fuck that. You're not sending Nicole to Flea Junction without some kind of back-up. You know Yarrow is a fucking punk."

"Nicole can handle herself," Badger said, shrugging.

I didn't like being talked about like I wasn't standing right there. I tucked the manilla envelope into my backpack. "Are you going to text me the address or sit around and bullshit for the next twenty minutes?"

"See? Nicole is a bad-ass now," Badger said with a smile that made him look like the Grim Reaper encouraging someone to take their own life. "Besides, Yarrow isn't going to fuck with Nicole because he knows if he does, I'll have his balls for lunch."

"Yarrow is an idiot. Self-preservation doesn't occur to him until after he's done fucked up. He tried to mess with Nova, and Nova was your sister."

"And he paid for that mistake," Badger returned, stubbing out his cigarette. "To my knowledge, he hasn't disrespected me since...unless you know something, I don't?"

I looked at Dylan. "I'll be fine. Stay here. I'll be back to pick you up."

I would've thought that Dylan would've stayed willingly with Badger seeing as she had a secret thing for the criminal, but she wasn't going to be left behind. To Badger, she said, "Fuck you. I'm going." She shouldered her pack, adding with a curl of her lip, "And take a fucking shower or something. You smell like you died."

Only Dylan could talk to Badger like that, but then membership into their tight, dysfunctional little club had its privileges.

Badger took an exploratory sniff at his pits and grinned. "Smells like perfection to me."

"Yeah, if perfection is smelly cheese and toe-fungus," Dylan quipped as we walked out of the office.

"You didn't need to come," I said. "I'm not an infant."

"Yeah, you're a bad-ass now," Dylan said with derision. "Look, you don't know what the streets are really like, especially the ones Badger runs. These people are just as likely to slit your throat and take the clothes off your back as any other motherfucker out there, but Yarrow is a slippery one. He's not like Badger. He comes off like he's the nice guy in this story, but let me tell you, he's got a heart as black, if not blacker than Badger. No one should go alone when heading to Flea Junction."

I digested that information, accepting the advice. I didn't know this world like Dylan, but I was a fast learner.

"Fine," I said but added, "I don't like you babying me. Just tell me straight how the lay of the land is, and I'll listen. If you try to baby me, I'll shut you out."

"Fair enough," Dylan said with grudging respect, falling into step with me as we hit the streets.

Having Dylan as my wingman was a good idea. She knew the ins and outs of running for Badger, as well as the temperaments of the players. As far as anyone else was concerned, I was fresh meat surrounded by hungry predators.

But this freshie wasn't playing around. I would learn anything I could from these people. Skills I couldn't get in a classroom.

Yeah, everyone had a reason for doing things.

Including me.

2

Weeks of running jobs for Badger had enabled me to build a nice stash of cash for myself. There were times when I looked at those crumpled bills, and I wondered what would happen if I did what Jilly had wanted us to do...leave New York and all of its bull-shit behind.

During rare moments of wild fantasy, I closed my eyes and pictured a life where I wasn't being hunted, where I wasn't kept from pursuing a future, where my friends weren't in danger of being clocked out for merely knowing me.

But what I told Jilly then still holds true now — Madame Moirai would never stop trying to find us because we were dangerous loose ends that she couldn't afford.

I mean, it wouldn't do to have the merch fighting back, right? We were just product to move around, use until we were broken, and then toss away.

Auction girls didn't get to run off and live their best life. They had to serve until they dropped dead, their mouths silent forever.

God, I hated that fucking woman.

After that reminder sunk home, I would tuck away my money box and prepare for another night on the streets after Hicks passed out.

Some days I heard him snoring early. Other days, like today, it seemed he tried to fight the urge to drown himself in hooch, and it took a bit longer.

A knock at the door surprised me. What was more surprising was how quickly Hicks was up from his desk, gun at the ready as he barked from behind the door, "Who is it?"

"Pope," the muffled answer followed.

Hicks returned the gun to his belt holster and unlocked the door. Kerri, the NYPD detective on our side, walked in carrying groceries.

Not gonna lie, I was hungry, and the sight of those bags was welcome.

"What the hell is this?" Hicks grumbled, dropping back into his desk chair, eyeing Kerri with irritation. "I don't need you to do my grocery shopping."

"I told you, if you're going to have two kids in your apartment, you have to feed them," she returned, unloading the bags. "Besides, it looks like you could use some real food, too. You're looking like shit, Hicks."

"I get my beauty sleep when I need it," Hicks said.

"You'd have to sleep until you're dead to make up for that hot mess," Dylan said, pointing in his overall direction. "You look like you're eighty years old already." She paused a minute, then asked, "How old are you, exactly?"

"Old enough to know that I shouldn't insult the guy letting me stay rent-free in his spare bedroom."

I laughed and shrugged when Dylan looked to me for back-up. I guess the booze hadn't totally pickled his brain yet.

Kerri chuckled and tossed Dylan a chocolate bar, her favorite. Dylan grunted her thanks, but I could tell Dylan was touched by Kerri remembering what she liked. When you were used to people treating you like you were an afterthought, it was hard to know how to react when people were actually friendly.

In most cases, it made you suspicious of their

motives, but in Kerri's case, she'd proven herself trustworthy.

Not to be forgotten, Kerri tossed my favorite candy to me. I caught it with a happy grin and tore into it.

She pulled a huge hero sandwich from the bag and began slicing. "I figured this was the best and easiest way to put some real food in your guts without having to cook something."

"Sounds good to me," I said, swiping two huge slices and joining Dylan on the couch. She accepted the piece and took a big bite. Between swallows, I asked, "Hey, anything on that mortuary yet?"

"Actually, yeah. That's why I came by."

"I thought you came by to bring us food," Dylan said with her mouthful.

"Killing two birds with one stone," Kerri said, bringing Hicks a sandwich slice, and when he tried to deny it, she pushed it at him with a determined look. "You need to eat. Your gut is probably bleeding from the inside out with all that booze you pour down your throat. I need you focused."

"I got what I need, right here," he said, lifting the bottle of Jack, but he sighed and took a grudging bite, only to complain, "This has mustard on it."

"Yeah? Deal with it," Kerri said. "So, I put in for

a records requisition at City Hall, looking for title ownership on the mortuary weeks ago, but I still haven't heard anything, which is weird. That's a simple paper trail that should be easy enough to get. Still, I got some excuse about cut-backs and limited staff for searches like this, and told it could be months before anyone got back to me."

"That seems excessive," Hicks grunted, taking another bite. "You think someone is stone-walling you?"

"Possibly. I mean, the city has had some cut-backs but to this level? I don't know...seems fishy."

"Sounds like bullshit to me. All those records are probably on a computer somewhere. All you gotta do is punch in the right search terms," I said, biting into my sandwich with a glower. "I'm getting real tired of this bitch covering every last trace of her trail with all this fucking red tape."

Kerri agreed. "One thing is for sure, they don't seem to leave anything to chance. They are more organized than I would like to see for a human trafficking network, but it also tells me that they've got tentacles everywhere."

"We already knew that," Dylan grumbled. "Whoever this bitch is, she's a fucking genius. Kinda like Badger, if you think about it."

"Yeah, good thing, Badger is on our side," I said.

"Badger isn't on anyone's side but his own," Dylan reminded me. "You need to stop thinking about Badger like he's looking out for us out of the goodness of his heart. The man would gut us both in a heartbeat without losing a moment's sleep if it benefited him."

I waved away her warning. "Yeah, yeah, Badger is bad. I get it. But if he's so bad, why do you have a hard-on for the guy? Either you're trying to make him look worse than he is, or you have really questionable taste in men."

"I don't have a thing for Badger," Dylan refuted with a dark look. "Shut your pie-hole about shit you know nothing about."

I rolled my eyes, too happy with my sandwich to fight with Dylan about her bullshit. Whatever, it didn't really matter to me if Dylan was into Badger because I wasn't. I didn't feel anything these days. The idea of feeling anything remotely sexual turned me into a frigid nun. Someday, if I lived to run into this problem, I'd probably have to find a way to unpack that box, but for now, it wasn't necessary.

I was hyper-focused on finding the assholes that ruined my life.

"So, what do we do if they keep stalling us on the record search?" I asked.

"I might have someone who can get us access to the records in a different way. Let me work on that first. I wanted to give the traditional channels a chance to work."

"That's a waste of time," Dylan groused. "That bitch is going to run circles around you and laugh while you fall on your face. We need to do things guerilla-style. The rules don't apply anymore."

"Look, I know it's hard, but we have to stay focused on the big picture—"

"I don't care about anything but making sure Madame Moirai chokes on her own blood," Dylan interrupted.

"Yeah, well, vengeance can be satisfying, but it doesn't last. If we really want to get results that matter, we have to rip apart the network, so they never do this again. For all we know, Madame Moirai is just a figurehead and not the mastermind. If we only remove the head from the cockroach, it can still run around, but if we squash it beneath our boot, it ain't going nowhere. Understand?"

Dylan didn't want to agree, but Kerri made sense. "Yeah, fine, but if she ain't playing by the rules, you can't expect to beat her by following a traditional playbook."

"The kid's got a fair point," Hicks said, wiping his mouth. "Unlike you, I got information on the house in Esterdell."

I perked up. "Yeah? Like what?"

"Purchased in 2010 for a couple mil in cash, title registered under a shell company."

"What does that mean?" I asked.

"It means the buyers used cash funneled through an inactive company so they could purchase anonymously with no bread crumbs leading back to the purchaser."

"I don't even know what the fuck that means, but it sounds like more rich people perks," Dylan quipped. "If you have enough money, you don't have to take responsibility for anything."

I was learning that lesson real quick. "So, what's the name of the shell company?"

"Avalon Incorporated."

My jaw dropped. "Seriously? And you're just now telling us this? Isn't this is a big win? We have their paper trail now."

"Hold up, kid. If only it were that easy. When I looked up the articles of incorporation through the

Secretary of State portal, I found that the shell company was registered under a false name."

"What was the name?" Kerri asked, frowning.

"Robert Jones."

"No points for originality," I quipped. "Why not, John Smith? Or Bob White?"

Dylan snickered but followed with, "Hold up, how is it that no one is paying attention to the details in these big city and state departments? I mean, is it so easy to just lie on official documents and shit? I can't even get a freaking driver's license because I don't have a social security card or a birth certificate, but these fuckers can create entire companies out of thin air? It's not fucking fair."

"The world works a lot differently for regular folk," Kerri said, shaking her head. "Money talks, and people listen. I wish it were different. I would love to say that the law is the law, and it's applied equally to rich or poor, but we all know that's not true."

"Yeah, preaching to the choir," Dylan said. "Just sucks, you know?"

"It does." Kerri looked to Hicks. "Did you find anything else that might help?"

"Not yet, still running down attachments. They had to use someone's social security number even if they used a made-up name to attach to it, but finding that person is like looking for Waldo."

"Who's Waldo?" Dylan asked, confused.

"That cartoon guy with the weird, goofy glasses and funky shirt," I quickly explained. Sometimes I forgot that Dylan left home at eleven, which hadn't left a lot of room for education, pop culture, or anything resembling normal kid stuff.

Not that I had a sunny childhood either, but at least Carla put a roof over my head. I would give her that much.

Speaking of Carla..."You still planning to talk with my mom?" I probably shouldn't have asked, but I couldn't help myself. "I mean, I don't care, but it might be useful to find out what she knows."

In a suspicious show of maternal behavior, my mom made a big production on social media, crying and pleading with people to help bring me home. In a normal situation, that would seem an appropriate response, but my mom wasn't a candidate for Mother of the Year.

We needed to find out what she knew and if Madame Moirai had promised Carla a big payday if she handed me over.

"Yeah, I'm glad you mentioned it. I think it's time to see if your mom is in contact with anyone that might lead us to The Avalon, but you can't come with me."

"You won't know if she's lying," I said.

"But if you show up and she's getting paid for information on you, it'll put you in danger," Kerri said.

"You could wear a wire and have the kid on a headset," Hicks suggested. "I could be around the corner. Like the old surveillance days."

"That's not a bad idea," Kerri said. "I could get some equipment easy enough. My captain put me on some bullshit drug surveillance. I could use that as the reason for the equipment requisition." She looked at me. "Are you open to doing that?"

"Yeah," I answered, feeling weird, though. I hadn't seen my mom since I left with Mr. Personality. Just watching her on that Facebook Live clip made my stomach clench with an unfamiliar sensation. I wouldn't call it grief or sadness, but it definitely hurt nonetheless.

I read once that no matter what adults put them through, abused kids still loved their parents and wanted to forgive them. At the time, I'd thought the statement was total bullshit, but maybe it wasn't crap after all. I guess that tiny part of me that still hoped my mom would stop being an asshole and actually care about me wasn't as dead as I'd hoped.

Pretty damn pathetic, honestly.

All I could say was I hoped we got some good intel for the gut punch that was coming my way; otherwise, the pain would be a waste.

Pain with a purpose seemed easier to swallow, I guess.

The lies we tell ourselves, right?

3

Dylan opted out of the plan to sit in Hicks' smelly car as we listened with earbuds to Kerri talk to my mom. I didn't ask what she was going to do. I assumed she was going to find herself hanging with Badger. For all her protests, she spent a lot of time around him, but that was her business, not mine.

My stomach clenched against the greasy breakfast burrito I'd slammed from a street vendor before heading out. Jesus, I should've known better. My gut had always been my Achilles heel. Nerves gave me diarrhea. Right now, I needed a bathroom, bad.

Hicks noticed my squirming in the seat and said, "You got ants in your pants, kid?"

"I'm about to shit myself," I muttered, closing my

eyes against the wave of pain twisting my intestines. "I think that burrito was bad."

He grunted as if he understood without me having to admit I was nervous. He swung onto a side street and pointed at a bodega. "There's a bathroom in there. I know the owner, and he's cool. If anyone asks, just tell them you're a friend of Hicks'."

I didn't wait on the offer. I bailed from the car and ran into the store, mumbling, "I'm a friend of Hicks, can I use your toilet?" and the man behind the counter handed me a key attached to a cinder block, pointing toward the back.

I slammed the bathroom door shut, locking it, and barely managed to get my pants down before I embarrassed myself.

As my guts unloaded, I cradled my head in my hands, hating that Carla had this effect on me even when she wasn't around. I never should've eaten that burrito knowing I was going to hear her voice again.

My entire childhood Carla had been an abusive twat, but there'd been times, small slivers of time that barely made a ripple in my memories when she'd been decent.

More like a parent should be.

I remembered one time before my Gran died

that my mom had gone through this period of trying to get her life straightened out.

I guess she'd met this guy — a man had always been the catalyst for any change in my mom's life — and he'd been unlike the rest. *Nice*, I guess? *Decent*? More like a normal person who wasn't out to ruin another person's life just to get laid, you know? Maybe my mom had wanted to be a better person for him.

And she really tried. At first.

She smiled a lot more. I remember that.

I also remember thinking that my mom was actually kinda pretty when she wasn't screaming and throwing things at me.

I barely remembered the guy's face or his name, but I remembered the day the veneer shattered.

My mom had been trying to kick the booze, but she was sneaking sips here and there when Mr. Perfect wasn't around. That night she'd had a few too many drinks, I guess. When he came over, dinner was burning on the stove, my mom was a sloppy drunk, and then the screaming started.

He must've realized he didn't have the energy to deal with whatever she was throwing out there and bailed.

I never saw Mr. Perfect again.

And I never really saw my mom's happy face again, either.

The only bright spot in that point of time was when Carla went off the deep end for a while, she'd had the decency to drop me off with Gran and disappear for weeks at a time, doing God-only-knew-what.

My mom was too fucking damaged to hold onto anything worth having. She was the queen of self-destruction.

I didn't know what had broken her, but there was no putting those pieces back together again.

I roused myself from the hurt locker of my childhood memories and flushed the toilet. I washed my hands, feeling bad for whoever had to follow me after I'd destroyed that bathroom. I returned the cinder block key and hustled out of the store.

I climbed into the car, saying, "I hope I didn't just ruin your friendship with the store owner. I think I might've died in there."

"Don't worry about it, kid." Hicks chuckled and pulled back into traffic.

I smiled to myself. It was too bad Hicks was a drunk, too. Unlike my mom, Hicks was a pretty decent guy. At least he didn't take out his demons on the people around him. That was saying something in my book.

As we got closer to my old neighborhood, my throat threatened to close. There was nothing about my old hood that should've smacked of nostalgia, and yet, my eyes were filling.

I wiped away the tears with the sleeve of my jacket, thankful that Hicks didn't ask me if I was all right. Clearly, I wasn't.

We were about a block away from my apartment. Hicks parked and pulled the equipment from the case, handing me a set of earbuds before placing his own and adjusting the volume. He texted Kerri that we were ready. Kerri responded that she was about five minutes out, which gave us a few minutes to watch the cars go by.

The inner city had a rhythm all its own, a savage urban jungle beat that held people hostage or set them free. People watching had always fascinated me. God knew I'd spent more than half my life, observing from a dirty stairwell.

"You love this shit, don't you?" I asked.

"Which shit?"

I pointed to the fancy earbuds. "Cop shit."

"Sometimes."

I smiled, hearing the truth in the lie, but that was okay. We all lied to ourselves when something was too raw to accept. Hicks was a broken man who'd lost everything that'd ever meant anything to him. This was probably the closest he'd ever come to getting that good feeling again. "Do you ever...try to talk to your kid?"

He cleared his throat, shrugging. "She's better off without me mucking up her life."

"You miss her, though, right?"

"Everyday."

He could've told me to fuck off and stop talking about personal, painful shit, but I think he must've sensed that I needed to hear something that reaffirmed that I wasn't the only one being fucked by life.

Kerri's voice sounded in my ear with a little static as she readjusted her wire. Video feed popped up seconds later. Kerri's rig was high-tech. Not only was she wired for audio, but the button pin in her shirt provided a visual feed. "Radio silence from this point forward," she said in a low tone before she knocked. We knew Carla was home because Kerri had watched her movements for a few days. Since Carla wasn't working — she lost her job because she was too busy looking for me, *yeah right* — she spent most of her days getting shit-faced drunk or heading out to get more booze. Carla was living her best life without me around to get in the way.

Kerri knocked again, and a boozy Carla answered. "Who are you?" she asked with suspicion. "What do you want?"

I stared at the video feed, my gaze narrowing at the sight of the woman I detested most. She looked like hell. Her hair was a rat's nest on top of her head. Her skin looked sucked of all moisture, adding at least ten extra years to her face. Hard to believe at one time, my mom had been quite the looker.

Now she just looked tired, hard, and old.

"My name is Det. Kerri Pope, I'm with the NYPD, here to talk to you about your daughter, Nicole. May I come in?"

"Did you find her?" Carla asked her expression sharpening with interest. "Where is she?"

"May I come in?" Kerri repeated with calm, dispassionate detachment.

"I guess, but I wasn't exactly expecting company, okay?" Carla muttered, glancing around the pig-sty she lived in. I could almost smell the apartment through the video feed. "Otherwise, I would've picked up or something."

Carla could give two shits about the state of the apartment. If anyone had ever done any cleaning, it'd been me. Since I'd been gone, it was apparent she hadn't lifted a damn finger to clean up her own mess.

Pizza boxes and Chinese take-out littered the countertops, and the sink overflowed with dirty dishes. A steady drip of water from the leaky faucet splashed on the teetering plates and glasses. *I guess some things never change.* Carla remained a slovenly pig with the lowest of standards.

"I don't have anything to offer you but tap water," Carla said, shrugging. "Some of us ain't living high on the hog, if you know what I mean."

"Thank you. I'm fine. May I sit?"

"Be my guest. It's not like I'm the queen of England or nothing."

Kerri settled onto the old, lumpy sofa that'd always smelled like stale cigarettes and wet dog, giving an excellent view of Carla in all her magnificent, horrid glory. I slid my gaze away in embarrassment, catching Hicks' eye. He shook his head as if to say, 'Fuck her' and 'good riddance,' and it all but broke the dam open that I was holding back with willpower and tape. Swallowing the lump in my throat, I returned my attention to the feed as soon as Kerri started talking again.

"So, about your daughter...we saw the Facebook Live video you posted, but I noticed your social media presence before that video was pretty nil. In fact, the date of creation is the same day you posted the video. My guess is that you're not exactly social media savvy. Did you have help setting up the video?"

Carla shifted in the chair opposite Kerri, grabbing a nearly crumpled pack of cigarettes, looking for a fresh one. "Didn't seem that hard. I figured it out myself," she answered, irritated that the pack was empty. She started rooting around for another pack on the messy coffee table. "You cops ain't doing shit to find my Nicole, so I figured, I'd better do what I can to get the word out."

"When did you report your daughter missing?" Kerri asked.

"Well, I mean, I didn't know she was missing right away if that's what you're asking. The girl runs off all the time. I thought she was just hanging with that rich little friend of hers, Lora-something-or-another. She thinks I don't know that she's ashamed of her family, well, she's wrong. Mothers know their daughters."

"Were you close?"

I held my breath. Carla found a cigarette. The *snick* and *snap* of a lighter as she lit up was the only sound before she answered with a subtle squint. "Close? Not exactly. I mean, I tried, but nothing's ever good enough for Nicole, you know? Hard to get close to someone who ain't interested in letting you in."

Anger heated my cheeks. "Give me a fucking break," I muttered, shaking my head. I hoped Kerri saw through Carla's act because this was pure fiction. My childhood was nothing but a series of bruises and confusion. I wanted to reach through the monitor and rip her scraggly hair out.

Hicks sensed my rage and pressed his finger to his lips. We couldn't distract Kerri.

I glanced away, shaking my head, but I remained quiet.

"Teenagers are hard to reach," Kerri commiserated. "So I'm guessing you called her friend Lora to see if Nicole was with her, and that's how you discovered that Nicole was missing?"

"Yeah, yeah, that's how it went."

I wanted to shout, 'Carla didn't have Lora's phone number.' but I ground my teeth in silence, listening.

"Let me just back up a minute...you said you called her friend, Lora...do you happen to have that number handy? I'd like to follow up."

"Why? I told you she didn't know where Nicole was."

"Yeah, I just have to do the leg work, paper trail, and all that."

"Well, I don't fucking remember her number, and I didn't keep it."

Kerri paused. "You didn't think it was wise to hold onto the number?"

"Don't fucking judge me, cop. My daughter is missing. I'm the victim here. Try to remember that."

"Seems to me that Nicole is the victim," Kerri returned.

"Yeah? Well, so am I." Carla sniffed, offended. "Look, if you're not here to tell me you've found my daughter, you can get the fuck out. I don't have to put up with this kind of harassment and judgment from you. You got kids?"

"No."

"Yeah, I didn't think so. Then you don't know what it's like to have your own flesh and blood go missing."

"You're right. I don't," Kerri agreed, her tone remaining the same despite Carla's turning shrill. "I'm just trying to understand how a grieving, distraught mother doesn't hold onto her daughter's best friend's phone number." She paused a minute, adding, "Unless you never actually talked to this friend, and you got the information from someone else..."

"Someone else? Like who?"

"I don't know. You tell me. Who set up the donation page for you? I saw you had a sizable donation from an anonymous donor...any idea who that might've been?"

"No," Carla answered with an edge. "That's the whole point of it being anonymous. Someone with a big heart, I guess."

"Carla...can I be frank with you?" Kerri didn't wait for Carla to answer. "Here's the thing, I don't think you set up that donation page. I think someone did it for you. Probably the same person who made the hefty donation. Why don't you just tell me who did you a solid and give me their contact information."

"What makes you think I have their number?"

I smiled at how deftly Kerri had manipulated Carla into revealing the truth behind her lies.

"Call it a hunch," Kerri said.

"I don't understand what the big deal is. Being nice to someone during a shit time isn't a fucking crime."

"Nope, of course not. But doesn't it seem a little odd? Why would some benevolent stranger appear to help you create a social media account and a donation site out of the blue? Had you ever met this person before? C'mon, let's be real, you don't seem like a people person, am I right?"

"Fuck off."

"Yeah, but first, I need answers, and I need you to stop wasting my time and lying to me."

"I'm not lying."

"You are, and I want the name and contact information of whoever is behind the benevolence."

"Jesus, at least he's interested in finding my Nicole, not like you cops."

"Either you're a shit mother, or you're too stupid to realize that a strange man coming around to offer you money to find your kid that he's never met is up to no good."

"What are you talking about? Is Nicole in some kind of trouble?"

"Well, she *is* missing — that in itself seems like she might be in danger. Give me a name and contact number, Ms. West."

"He wanted to stay anonymous."

"Yeah, well, people in hell want ice water, too."

I grinned. Hicks' expression was pure respect. Kerri had twisted Carla around without breaking a sweat, and it was beautiful. All those times, my mom had bullied or lied her way out of consequences faded away in the brilliance of Kerri's efficient takedown.

"I'm not the best mom, but I'm not the worst, either," Carla said, picking at her cuticle as if Kerri had managed to find the tiniest bit of her capable of feeling shame. "I mean, I love the little shit, you know? But I think she's done something real stupid, and this guy just wants to help bring her home."

"Is that what he said?"

"Well, no, but I just got that vibe. I'm good at reading people. He seemed to really care. I mean, who puts up that kind of money for a stranger's kid?"

"No one good," Kerri answered. "That number, please."

Carla nipped at her cuticle, wincing as the dried skin peeled a little too far. "Here's the thing, he said I had to keep it quiet. He's been really good about keeping my bills paid 'cause he knows I can't work right now. I don't want him to think I ain't grateful."

And there it was — it was all about the money. That's all it'd ever been about.

I heard the disgust in Kerri's voice as she repeated, "The number please, Ms. West."

I pulled the earbuds from my ear and looked away from the video monitor.

Madame Moirai had gotten to my mom — and the bitch had been more than willing to sell me out.

My eyes stung, and my chest burned.

From this moment forward, Carla West was dead to me.

4

Kerri gave Hicks the number so he could run it down. She couldn't risk going through regular channels to trace the call without throwing up alarms, especially since her lieutenant had been giving her side-eye lately.

Every time she tried pushing toward the missing girl angle, he shut her down with a terse, 'Stop chasing dead ends' and she had no choice but to back off while on duty.

Hicks didn't suffer the same kind of scrutiny, and his channels weren't quite as scrupulous, but they were effective. Just when I thought Hicks' bag of tricks was empty, he came up with something new, which was exactly what we needed when we were outgunned, outmanned and basically, fucked.

To say we were the underdogs was a gross understatement.

So while Kerri dodged her lieutenant, Hicks worked with us behind the scenes using every tool in his arsenal. I didn't really care who got the job done. I was interested in results.

"Hold onto your butts," Hicks said, preparing to make the call. My hands were sweaty, and Dylan was practically vibrating with tension beside me even though she didn't say a word. We had no idea who was on the other side of that phone, but we knew they were connected to Madame Moirai.

Hicks' connection had set him up with a machine that tracked the cell tower ping, which then triangulated the approximate location of the caller. We knew this was a burner phone, so it wasn't going to be exact, but it would help.

Hicks made the call, motioning for us to be silent as he put the phone on speaker.

One ring. Two rings. A click.

"Ms. West, so happy to hear from you. I'm assuming you've made contact with Nicole?"

I stiffened in recognition as my gaze flew to Dylan's. Her expression mirrored mine.

We knew that voice, but I only knew him as Mr.

Personality, the man who'd facilitated the bullshit contract and ferried us to the auction house.

"Sorry, not Ms. West, whoever that may be...I found this phone and was trying to find the owner. There was only one number in the recent call list, and you were it. I was hoping you could help me out so I could get the phone to the rightful owner. I know I'm lost without my phone. I'd hate for someone else to go through that if they don't have to, you know what I mean?"

The bullshit flowed so easily from Hicks' mouth. I was impressed. The whole point was to keep Mr. Personality talking so the tracing program could do its magic.

But Mr. Personality wasn't playing. The line went dead.

Disappointment dragged my shoulders, but I dared to hope, "Did you get anything?" When Hicks cursed under his breath and bounced his pencil across the desk, I knew he hadn't. *Goddamn it, couldn't we get a fucking break?*

Dylan rose and grabbed her jacket, saying, "I need some air" and left the apartment. Maybe she'd pinned more hope on that call than even I had. Dylan wasn't one to share her feelings, good or bad, but I could feel the hopelessness rolling off her in waves.

"That was our one shot, wasn't it?" I asked.

"Likely, he smashed that phone and tossed it the minute he realized it wasn't your mother on the other line."

"We should've played along. Maybe if I'd answered," I said, frustrated, "he would've stayed on the line long enough to catch."

"And that would've just given away your position and put you and Dylan into more danger. No, this was the only play, and it just didn't pan out as we'd hoped," Hicks answered, reaching for the bottle of Jack. "Don't worry, kid. We'll get another chance."

But I was worried. So far, our luck hadn't been great in the chance department. Madame Moirai was pretty damn good at setting up traps. She'd already snagged my worthless mother, what if she got to Lora, too? Should I try to warn her? The last time I tried to talk to Lora about my situation, she'd thought I was bonkers and being needlessly dramatic.

I couldn't say I blamed her. If I hadn't experienced the situation, I would've been skeptical, too. Logically, I knew that there was nothing I could say to Lora that would make her believe my story, which meant there was nothing I could do to save her either. I blinked back tears. I couldn't stand the thought of Lora getting hurt because of me, but I had zero control over anything, so I wasn't in a position to do much more than worry.

And even though I resisted the feeling, I realized my mom was probably in danger, too.

"What about Carla?" I asked, hating myself for feeling anything for that lying cunt, but I guess it was imprinted on my brain to care at some level, even if it was buried beneath the concrete. "If Mr. Personality knows that my mom talked to Kerri, and that's how we got the number..."

But Hicks wasn't going to let me go there. "Something tells me your mom is a survivor. She'll be fine."

"Yeah, you're probably right. Cockroaches always find a way to survive."

"So I take it, you recognized the voice?" Hicks asked.

"Immediately," I said, without a doubt. "I can't explain it, I just knew. So did Dylan. I nicknamed him Mr. Personality because he didn't seem to have one. He was dry, to-the-point, and showed zero emotion. He was the one who put together the so-called legal aspects of the deal and then took us to the auction house. I never saw him again after that.

Honestly, I don't even know why I recognized his voice so quickly."

"Vivid memories are tied to emotional experiences," Hicks explained. "So, are you saying you'd recognize his voice anywhere?"

"I think so."

"That's good to know."

"But that was our one and only real lead," I said, dropping on the couch. "Now what?"

"I was thinking, I had a rich client one time, wanted me to catch his wife fucking some art gallery guy. In my experience, the one percent love a chance to spend their money, strutting around like a bunch of peacocks, tossing their cash around like they've got more than the next guy."

"Like how?"

"Art showings, gallery openings, hoity-toity fundraisers for politicians at a-thousand-bucks-a-plate," Hicks answered with a shrug. "Anything where they can get dressed up in designer crap, eat like birds, and feel superior around their own little cliques."

"Yeah, I get that, but how are we supposed to get an invitation to stuff like that? We're not exactly rolling in the Benjamins."

"True, but if you know what to look for, you can find just about anything or anyone on social media."

"Sure, if you've got a name," I grumbled, "which we don't."

"Sometimes, you luck out with a situation that looks ripe. Take a look at this," he said, waving me over to his laptop, where he cued up a social media page for some ritzy event. "A fundraiser is happening in a few days where the Head of Social Services, Bitsy Aldridge is going to be the keynote speaker. This is a strictly A-list kind of crowd. My money is on someone connected to this Avalon Inc is going to be there."

"Yeah, makes sense, but it's not like they're going to put that information on their name tag," I said. "I wish there was some kind of identifying mark they had to wear that showed the world what kind of piece of shit they were."

"Kid, the world would collapse if that were possible. Lies, and the ability to hide your true self, is the sacred tool in a human being's tool chest."

"It's fucked up."

"No argument from me. Just saying, everyone lies — whether to themselves or others. Fact of life."

He was right. "Still sucks," I muttered. "And for the record, I don't lie. What you see is what you get."

"You're lying to yourself that you don't care about your mom," he said.

I scowled. "No, I'm not."

"It's okay to admit that you're worried about her. She may be a shit person, but that doesn't mean you are. Caring about others isn't a bad thing. Never get that twisted, kiddo."

I blinked back sudden tears. My throat closed up. I wasn't a hugger, and neither was Hicks, but somehow I felt like he'd just given me a psychic hug, and I didn't know how to deal with it.

Thankfully, Hicks sensed my struggle and kept moving forward. "So what we need to do is get a confirmed guest list and start running the names."

I wiped at my eyes, grateful to refocus. "Can you do that?"

"Everything is electronic these days. I might know someone who can get us a digital copy of the list."

"Then what? If we don't know the real names of anyone, how will we know that they're connected?" I asked, confused.

"I ain't saying it's a sure thing, but sometimes you gotta scratch around before you hit pay dirt. We run the names through the search engines using the image function. If you see someone you recognize, we got 'em."

A frisson of wild hope dared to flare to life. Just as Mr. Personality's voice was burned into my memory, so was every person's face associated with my auction experience. Was it possible I might catch my buyer? I'd recognize that fucker in the dark. "Do it," I said. "We don't have anything to lose at this point, right?"

Hicks' subtle grin was everything. "Thatta girl."

For a moment, I saw the man he might've been if circumstances had been different in his life. Strong, smart, capable and shrewd — he'd probably been a kick-ass detective at one time. He didn't shy away from looking outside of the box for answers, and he wasn't afraid of bending the rules to get shit done.

If it weren't for the strong smell of booze on his breath and his bloodshot eyes, you'd never know he was about a half-hour away from being completely sauced.

Hell, no one was perfect. Sometimes the hero of the moment wasn't the guy wearing the white suit. He was the drunk with the heart of gold.

Given the fact my life had been spent thus far with the absence of anyone resembling a good guy, I'd take what I could get.

I was beginning to realize it wasn't reality that got us down, it was the picture in our head that told us the way life was supposed to be that really fucked us up.

Before the auction, I'd spent most of my energy trying to reach the promised land that leaving for college with Lora was supposed to be, but even in my most intense determined moments, I'd known...it was never going to measure up.

Maybe in some fucked up way, the auction had opened my eyes. One thing was for sure, I'd never see the world the same again.

The death of my innocence had nothing to do with the loss of my virginity – it had everything to do with the realization that given enough rope and resources, people would feel free to do their absolute worst to another human being.

Before the auction, I never truly grasped how awful human beings could be.

Now I knew.

That's how my innocence died.

There was no price for what they took. Nothing would ever compensate me for what they ripped out of me.

If there was a God – and the jury was still out on that score – I prayed he had a special place in hell for people like those wrapped up with Avalon Inc.

In the meantime, I'd have to make do with a little good ol' fashioned street justice for my payback.

For Tana.

For Jilly.

For every girl, they stole, lost, and ruined.

Retribution was my name, and I was ready to play.

5

The following day, Hicks had business to do outside of the apartment, and Kerri showed up, telling us to grab our backpacks because we were going on a road trip.

Dylan resisted at first, but Kerri had a way of pushing past Dylan's surly mood by leaving no room for her to refuse — usually by bribing her with food. Dylan, for all her growl, was motivated by a free meal.

The dots were easy to connect. After all those years of living on the streets, the threat of hunger had to be a visceral memory. If someone she trusted was offering up food, it was stupid to refuse because the memory of going without was never far from her head.

I knew that Kerri was coming to get us because she didn't like the idea of us being in the apartment alone without Hicks' protection. The gesture was sweet given the fact that technically, both Dylan and I were murderers at this point.

However, I liked a free meal, too, so I grabbed my pack, and we followed Kerri out. We had sneaking around the city down to a science. We wore cheap wigs beneath hoodies, avoided the CCTV, and kept to the shadows at night. During the day, we did the same, only we avoided main streets and tried to use the back alleys as much as possible.

Kerri shut off her dashcam, so they never caught us in her vehicle. I never imagined my most trusted allies would become two adults I hadn't even known two months ago and a girl who never would've been my friend under normal circumstances.

And now, I trusted them with my life.

We couldn't exactly hop into a restaurant like ordinary people, so Kerri always ordered ahead so she could swing by, pick up, and bail.

I was privately delighted when I saw she'd ordered a deep-dish pizza from one of my favorite pizza places. I started to open the box, but she stopped me with a light slap on my hand, saying,

"Get your mitts out of there," and I pouted, closing the lid.

"That's kinda like torture, putting a pizza in my hands and then telling me not to eat it," I said.

"Just be patient," she said with a low chuckle as she took us outside of the city. I didn't mind that the pizza might be cold whenever we reached wherever we were going. Pizza was good, cold or hot. It was a relief to get out of the city and away from the apartment. Sometimes I felt mold growing in parts of my soul from the rot of the city seeping into my bones.

The countryside felt cleansing.

Also, there weren't any cameras or the threat of someone looking over our shoulder in the middle of nowhere.

I smiled for the first time in a while.

Even Dylan seemed more relaxed.

Kerri took us to a park along the river. We unloaded and found an old wooden bench that we commandeered for our picnic. Sunlight glinted off the river as the current kept the water moving, and birds circled in the sky, taking advantage of the nice day.

It was still cold as hell, but I didn't mind. We ate our pizza in easy silence, each of us locked in our own thoughts but enjoying the company. I didn't think I'd ever been so relaxed than at that moment. I was happy to simply eat pizza and think of nothing other than the fantastic burst of pleasure from my taste buds.

Sometimes food was like that — the best, most perfect manifestation of a good feeling.

Kerri broke the silence first. She wiped her mouth and sighed, looking out across the water. "You'd think that this place would be the last place on earth I'd ever revisit," she said.

Confused, I asked, "What do you mean? It seems nice."

She pointed at the banks. "That's where they pulled my little sister from the water."

I recoiled in horrified surprise. "Your sister?"

"Yeah, she'd gone missing when she was twelve. Two weeks later, a fisherman happened upon her body when it'd washed up on shore."

"Oh my God, that's awful." Suddenly the place didn't seem so idyllic. "Why do you come back here?"

"I know it's weird, but sometimes I feel connected to her here. When I feel lost or alone, sometimes I come, and I pretend that she's sitting here with me, watching the water, listening to the boats, or digging her feet in the sand." She wasn't offended by my dubious expression, but I couldn't imagine how she found comfort here. Kerri drew a deep breath, admitting, "Trust me, I know it sounds bonkers, but it works."

"That's fucked up," Dylan said, shaking her head. "You're nuts."

I shot Dylan a quelling look, and she shrugged as if she gave zero fucks, which she probably didn't. I tried offering some kind of condolence. "I can't say I understand, but I'm sorry about your sister. I can't imagine what that must've been like. What happened?"

"She was riding her bike home from school. I was supposed to go with her, but I stayed behind to hang out with friends. She never came home. Her disappearance was a shock to the community. We were just a small town where nothing ever happened. I didn't think twice about letting Trina go home alone. It seemed everyone joined the search party from the town, but we didn't find her until she washed up."

"That's morbid," Dylan said, wrinkling her nose, her gaze sliding to the water as if imagining the young girl's body. "If that'd happened in my past, I'd never step foot near this place."

"I felt that way for a long time. One day I found myself here, and everything was different. What happened was shitty. In an instant, my life changed, but it also made me who I am today. I became a cop because of what'd happened to Trina."

"Did they ever catch who killed her?" I asked.

Kerri shook her head. "Never did."

"That sucks," Dylan said. "I bet it drove your parents crazy."

"It did. Ruined their marriage. Nothing was ever the same after Trina died."

Dylan glanced away, voicing the same thought bouncing around in my head. "I'm sorry your sister died, but if you're about to say 'everything happens for a reason,' I'm going to peace out on that conversation. Shitty things happen, and it's random as fuck. Maybe you were always going to be a cop, and your sister didn't have to die for you to fulfill your fucking destiny, ever think of that?"

"Sure, you can think that," Kerri agreed, "or you can choose to believe that perhaps Trina's death helped me to save the lives of other little girls later. I spent years in the missing persons unit, and I helped bring home hundreds of people, from senior citizens to little kids, and that has to mean something, right?"

Dylan shrugged. "You can believe what you want. It's not in me to play that game. If you're saying all the shit I've been through was for some grand purpose or design, I say, fuck that, because I'm willing to bet there were a helluva lot better ways to accomplish the same goal than terrorizing a little kid and then having her live on the streets to survive. Yeah, fuck that. It's all bullshit, and there's no rhyme or reason to anything except that it's all a fucking crapshoot." She rose stiffly and walked down to the bank to sit on the cold, sandy beach. Kerri had touched a nerve, and Dylan wasn't comfortable with anyone seeing how deeply that pain went.

I wanted to apologize for Dylan, but she had only echoed what I was thinking. I wish I could apply some uplifting meaning to the shit I'd endured, but I couldn't. I felt the same as Dylan. Sometimes life was just random as fuck. If you had the misfortune to end up with the losing hand, that's how it went.

Still, I risked a glance at Kerri, saying, "Does it bother you that Trina's killer was never found?"

"Every day. Without closure, it's hard to put an end to your grief. This was how I found a way to move on. Before that, I was a mess. I put my parents through a lot before I realized how I needed to channel my anger."

"You were a hellion?" I asked.

"Yeah, you could say that. Let's just say I understand Dylan a lot better than she thinks."

"Yeah?" I was surprised. Kerri seemed the straight arrow that always flew true.

She nodded. "Which is why I want you guys to stop running jobs for Badger."

That was a battle I knew Kerri wouldn't win. Especially not with Dylan. "We need the money," I said, wiping at my hands even though they were clean. "I mean, it's not like we can just walk into a restaurant and apply for a waitressing gig. Even girls hiding from a clandestine sex trafficking ring have to eat," I said, trying for some light humor, but Kerri wasn't laughing.

"You're taking risks you don't need to take," she said. "Me and Hicks will make sure you're fed."

It wasn't just about the food. "I can't keep Dylan caged in that tiny apartment," I said, leaving out the part where I needed a change of scenery, too. "Have you ever seen a lion cooped up in a zoo? It ain't pretty. Besides, too much time with Hicks and Dylan makes me want to find Madame Moirai and surrender myself because all they do is pick at each other all day."

"Badger is bad news," Kerri persisted with concern. "That road is a dead end. Trust me."

I danced around her opinion. "He's not that bad. He helped us when no one else would. He's the reason we met Hicks. He can't be all that bad."

"He's a criminal, and he's only using you for what he can get out of you."

I shrugged. "Everyone has their faults."

Kerri's voice rang with frustration. "I need you to take this seriously. I can appreciate that Badger was the reason we met, but running jobs for him is only going to put you in danger, and that's the last thing we need right now. Nicole, you need to start thinking of your future. When this is all said and done, and we catch Madame Moirai, you can go back to your life. You won't be able to do that if Badger has you wrapped up in his illegal bullshit."

I barked a short laugh. "What life? I have nothing to go back to. It's not like I'm going to college like a normal kid and pretend like none of this ever happened."

"You can have a normal life if you choose. You're not like Dylan. You have a chance to put this all behind you. I'll help you. You're not alone."

"But what about Dylan? I can't just leave her. She needs me, and I'm not going to bail on her."

"I would never ask you to bail on Dylan. She's a

good kid with a good heart, but I fear her egg has too many cracks."

I scowled. "You don't know her like I do. We're a team, and I'm not going to abandon her."

Kerri must've realized I wasn't going to budge and backed down, but the seed had been planted. I didn't know what I was going to do if I survived this fight with The Avalon. A part of me believed I wouldn't live long enough to face the problem of a future. Survival took all the mental bandwidth I had. Living on borrowed time had a tendency to shorten the trajectory of your focus.

I didn't know what kind of life Dylan could possibly have beyond what Badger could provide, which meant Dylan was almost sure to be swept up into the life of crime that Badger lived.

I didn't necessarily want that for myself, but I would never leave Dylan to face an uncertain future alone. I also couldn't see Dylan living a normal life. I didn't know what to do, and I definitely didn't want to think about it.

"I'm really sorry about your sister." It was all I could offer. Promises were too expensive for someone who believed hope was too foreign a currency.

6

The Universe was definitely fucking with us. Kerri dropped us off at the end of the day, and Badger had a job for us later that night. After my conversation with Kerri, I felt a twinge of apprehension for accepting the gig, but like I told Kerri, Badger paid in cash, and we needed the money.

Except, this was no ordinary job. Badger was sending us to Diamond Lane — an area outside of his territory run by a man named King — which was definitely kinda fucked up on Badger's part because if King found out, their uneasy truce would shatter.

"What the fuck is he doing?" Dylan had muttered, giving the job the side-eye. "He knows King will start a war over this kind of shit."

I didn't know the backstory of King and Badger,

and I didn't want to know. The job seemed easy enough, even if it was in an area that was considered a no-fly zone for anyone in Badger's crew. I figured, if we got in, got out and left without drawing any attention to ourselves, we'd be golden.

But if it went sidewise? Fuck...I didn't want to think about it. Becoming collateral damage in a turf war seemed an ironic end to an already fucked up situation.

We slipped out of the apartment around midnight, dipping into the shadows and into the subway system. Dylan's vibe told me something was eating at her. I took a chance and poked around a little.

"Are you okay?"

"Yeah? Why wouldn't I be?"

"You haven't said much since Kerri dropped us off."

She shrugged. "Not much to say. I'm bored as fuck and riddled with anxiety, kinda stuck in the middle of that shit sandwich, you know?"

"Yeah, hard to know which way to go," I agreed, but I knew it was more than that. Kerri had thrown us for a loop with her confession. To lose a sister like that...hell, I didn't know what it was like to have a sibling, but after losing Jilly the way we did, I kinda had an idea. "I never would've guessed that Kerri had such a traumatic past."

Dylan didn't respond, she just kept walking. Both our minds were jacked-up places. I probably should've just left it alone but I couldn't. Maybe I needed to process, too.

"Got me to thinking...what if there is some big purpose to all this shit we've been through? I mean, what if Jilly and Tana died for a reason?"

Dylan shot me a dark look. I was treading on dangerous ground. "And Nova, too? And all those girls that are nothing but bones somewhere? Fuck that, you and I both know there's no reason. Just some messed up assholes who thought they were better than everyone else and thinking the rules don't apply to them."

"Maybe. I guess we'll never know until we kick the bucket and find out if there's an afterlife."

Dylan heaved an aggrieved sigh as if she didn't like to think about anything but the present moment and muttered, "Get your head on straight. Mistakes will cost you."

She was talking about the job with Badger. Of course, I knew she was right. I shouldn't be wasting time thinking about existential shit when we were running jobs. That's how people slipped up and ended up dead or worse, in the pit.

But Kerri's story had stuck in my head, clinging to my thoughts and leaving questions that couldn't be answered.

I saw the world differently these days. I felt as if two people were living inside my head: the person I was before the auction and the person I became after.

The person before still wanted to believe there was a chance at something better in life.

The person after didn't believe or trust in anyone.

As time wore on, I recognized less and less of the person before.

Dylan surprised me when she said, "You might've been shocked by Kerri's story, but I knew there had to be something that fucked her up."

"What do you mean, fucked up?" Kerri seemed the most level-headed adult I'd ever known, aside from Lora's parents, but they didn't count because they lived boring suburban lives. The biggest excitement in Lora's household was probably the decision to switch toilet paper brands.

"Because she's got a thing for Hicks, and he's as fucked up as they come."

"Yeah, so?"

"Don't you know what they say about birds of a feather? They stick to each other or something like that. My point is, she's holding a torch for a guy who's gonna do nothing but drag her down eventually because he ain't gonna change. He's a drunk and a deadbeat dad. He ain't changing that shit. He is what he is, but Kerri's holding onto the past, hoping he'll turn into the man he used to be, and that's never gonna happen. It's kinda sad, if you think about it."

I didn't like Dylan's judgment. I snapped back, "Sort of like you and Badger?"

Dylan snorted with sharp laughter. "What the fuck are you talking about? There's nothing between Badger and me."

"Yeah, I know, but you've got a thing for him. Everyone can see it. Except maybe you. And maybe Badger. It's as obvious as the nose on your face."

"I already told you, there's nothing between us," Dylan growled. "You're thick in the head."

"Whatever. You're willing to sell yourself short for a man who doesn't even see you as anything but a means to an end."

Dylan spun on her heel and hissed, "Yeah, well, we all sold ourselves, didn't we, *Nikki*? That's why we're in this mess, right? Just shut the fuck up. I'm tired of your judgy bullshit. You like to talk a big game like you're standing so tall above everyone else, but you're knee-deep in the shit pile like the rest of us. Stop acting like you didn't try to game the system because you did, and you're no less guilty."

I blinked at the sting. "I never said I didn't make the same mistake. I'm just saying..." What was I saying? The bubble rising in my throat tasted like hypocrisy. I shook my head and retreated. "Fuck it, never mind."

I thought that might be the end of it, but Dylan stepped into my personal space, her gaze two hot coals as she pinned me with a baleful stare. "Listen up and listen good. There ain't nothing between us, and there never will be. He's a dick, and he uses people. You think I can't see that? You think I'm blind to what Badger is? He's fucking sending us on a job that could go sidewise and leave us for dead. He likes to play with people, and no one is off-limits. Why the fuck do you think Nova made me promise not to tell him what she was doing? It was going to be her only way out. Badger was never going to let Nova go, no matter what he says. Badger only cares about one person — Badger. Nova wanted to be free of him. And I did, too. But here I am...still trapped under his fucking thumb. Don't come at me with shit you can't possibly understand, or I will fucking end you."

I was buffeted by the waves of impotent rage Dylan was throwing my way. At that moment, I was the stupid jerk for pressing buttons I knew I should've left alone. Sometimes my mouth was more than I could control. "I'm sorry," I murmured.

"Yeah, whatever." Dylan pulled her gaze away in disgust and started walking again.

Being trapped in a life, you couldn't escape — I understood that agony, even if it was dressed differently than the villain in my own nightmare.

And I was a dick for attempting to pass judgment from my glasshouse.

We trudged on in angry silence, winding our way through the crowds and popping up in the seedy neighborhood where we were supposed to make the delivery. Diamond Lane was the exact opposite of what the nickname implied. In fact, it wasn't a lane at all, it was an area where the transient population took refuge. The cops avoided Diamond Lane because it was a logistical nightmare and a paperwork headache, which created a perfect breeding ground for unsavory situations.

"Welcome to the jungle," muttered Dylan as her gaze darted, taking in the scene. "Let's just make the delivery and get the fuck out before someone sees us."

It was supposed to be a simple drop. We had a package from Badger and a drop-off point. We delivered, we got paid, we left. That was the plan.

But it seemed too much to ask of the Universe to let things go off without a hitch.

Dylan took point, I followed close behind her. Catcalls rang out in the night as we passed burning trash barrels and desperate people huddled by the fire for warmth.

Somewhere in the murky darkness, music played from a boom box, laughter rang out as random shots fired into the night sky. Our breath plumed in front of us as the flickering light from the fires created menacing shadows. I pulled my hoodie more tightly around my head and made sure to avoid eye contact with anyone.

Desperation had a vibe all its own. People who'd lost all hope and wallowed in their own destruction held little regard for anyone else. They became predatory and preyed on anyone they deemed weaker than themselves.

As fucked up as it was, this felt more honest than anything the Avalon did. At least here, no one was pretending to be anything more than what they were.

Sharks were expected in these waters, and you knew they would bite if you gave them a chance.

I respected that level of transparency, even if it was like trying to untangle razor wire with your bare hands.

I never imagined how dangerous Madame Moirai was when I signed that piece of paper. To think I'd actually thought I was being a badass, doing something so crazy as to sign away my virginity to pull myself out of the muck when in fact, I'd been walking right into the lion's den.

What a fucking joke.

"Up ahead," Dylan murmured for my ears only. A man leaning against the cement bridge support above our heads waited with sharp eyes and an air of menace that no one seemed to want to fuck with. We eyeballed the guy before Dylan asked flatly, "Tchaikovsky or Beethoven?"

"Beethoven is an overrated hack," the man answered.

Badger always required a password for his deliveries to ensure they were landing in the right hands. It wasn't like Badger could use an actual courier system for his product, so he had to improvise.

Dylan nodded and pulled the package from her backpack, which the man then stuffed in his own pack and disappeared into the inky darkness as if he'd never been there.

That was our cue to bail, too.

We started to hustle out, but our way was suddenly blocked by a group of thugs with stares as black as their souls.

"You lost?"

Dylan didn't flinch. "Nope. We were just leaving."

"I know your face," he said, folding his arms across his chest.

"Doubtful."

Cold fingers of dread climbed my spine. I remained rigid, tense, watching.

Dylan looked bored. "Your point?"

"You're one of Badger's crew," he said. "You're not supposed to be down here. You know the rules."

"Must've taken a wrong turn somewhere," Dylan said, shrugging. "Sue me."

He grinned, revealing a gold tooth. "Rule-breaker, huh? I like it. But here's the thing, King's got punishments for rule-breakers, and I'm here to make sure everyone colors inside the lines. You, little girl, just made a mess of things."

"You don't want to fuck with us," I warned, stepping closer to Dylan.

"Yeah? And why is that?"

I whipped a gun from my backpack, shocking the man and Dylan as I said, "Because I won't hesitate to splatter your DNA all over this fucking shit-hole of a place. Your call, asshole."

I thought the threat might be enough to cool his jets, but the man recovered quickly, his grin turning sly. "You can't kill us all." He started to slowly advance toward us. "And I doubt you have the balls to pull the trigger, sweetheart."

"Let's find out," I returned with a cold smile. "'Cuz, I came here kinda hoping a mother-fucker would."

7

Everything happened faster than I thought possible.

Faster than I could process what'd happened.

The thug rushed me, and I pulled the trigger. The acrid smell of gun powder burnt my nose. I tasted copper and sweat. I stumbled and fell on my ass as pandemonium erupted around us.

Someone tried to grab me. I kicked like a wild thing as I scrambled to my feet. I heard Dylan screech as she fought off her attacker. I swung and landed a hard punch to someone's face, and I kept scrabbling toward Dylan. She was kicking and shrieking like a banshee against the hold on her.

The man I'd shot remained motionless on the ground, blood seeping from the wound in his chest. I catapulted myself against Dylan's assailant and knocked them both to the ground.

Dylan rolled out of his grasp and popped to her feet. He caught her, sending her crashing to the ground again. She landed a vicious kick to his nose, sending blood everywhere. He let go, howling as he held his broken face.

Blood dribbled down my forehead from a gash I hadn't felt when it happened, and Dylan's lip was swollen. We were woefully outnumbered, just like the thug said we'd be.

I didn't have time to lament our sorry-ass luck. Suddenly, I was lifted from the ground from behind. Iron bands crushed my chest and squeezed the air from my lungs before I was slammed back to the ground. Dirt ground into my knee as my jeans ripped. Stars burst from behind my eyeballs as something hard hit me in the back of the head.

"Bitch, you gonna pay for what you done to Switch," a voice promised in my ear with rancid breath as hands tugged at my jeans, fumbling for my zipper. Panic pierced the fog in my brain as I struggled to get away. He called out after me, his voice mean, "Where you going, little girl? You think you can just waltz onto Diamond Lane when you wasn't invited?" as his blunt fingers dug into my thighs.

"Ohh yeah, baby, you gonna pay with that tight ass of yours. That's what you gonna do. Scream for me, baby girl. I like it."

He was going to rape me. Memories of my buyer paralyzed my body even as I tried to scream for help.

"Hurry up, D," a voice urged, "I want a turn, too."

My vision dimmed as a black-out threatened. The shrill peal of sirens cut through the ringing in my ears, and someone yelled out, "Cops!" sending people scattering like cockroaches scurrying away from the light.

I rolled to my knees with a groan and struggled to my feet. I turned to the sound of Dylan sucking in wild, gasping breaths as she coughed in the dirt, holding her neck where her skin was angry and raw.

"Cmon, let's go!" I motioned wildly, helping Dylan up as we used the distraction to run.

Our feet ate the pavement like the devil was on our heels. By the time we skidded into the subway terminal, barely making the next train, we were gasping, our lungs on fire.

We collapsed on the hard plastic seats, hearts thundering in our ears. The harsh light showed every bruise and swollen bit of skin covered in blood from scrapes and scratches we didn't remember getting.

My gaze swept the car. There were only a handful of unfortunate souls riding the train at this hour, and they didn't make eye contact.

Not that I blamed them. We were a mess, and no one wanted to screw around with drama that didn't involve them.

"What the fuck," I asked, breathing hard, my head pounding. I probably had a mild concussion. "What happened?"

Dylan winced as she repositioned herself. "King's crew made me. Fuck, this is going to start a war. This is all Badger's fault. He never should've sent us there. The fucker probably did it on purpose, hoping we'd get jumped."

My head was spinning, not only from the pain but from the shock of what'd just happened.

"Why would he do that?" I asked.

"Because he's a dick, and he likes to break his own fucking rules when he's in a mood."

"Then why'd we take this job?" I asked, my voice rising. Kerri was right. Badger was going to get us killed if we kept running jobs for him. He didn't fucking care if we got hurt as long as his bottom line didn't suffer.

"Because we did," Dylan shot back. "Jesus, you could've stayed behind if you didn't want to go."

"Yeah, and you would've been killed tonight if I hadn't come along," I returned, equally heated.

"Just shut up, okay? If I keep talking, I'm going to puke."

I moaned as a wave of pain made me double over. My ribs hurt where I must've taken a blow to the side. It hurt to breathe. *Possible fracture?* It wasn't like I could go to the hospital to find out.

Dylan whimpered in pain, something I never heard her do, and I lost my anger. "Are you okay?" I asked, blinking against my blurring vision.

"I'm fine," she croaked, but the pain radiating from her glazed eyes told a different story. We'd had our asses handed to us. If it weren't for that bust, we'd be dead.

Like the guy I killed.

I shuddered, the memory of the shot ringing in my ears. I realized with a start, I'd left the gun behind.

Sweat broke out across my body. I had to tell Kerri. If this wasn't the biggest fuck up to support her opinion, I didn't know what was.

"Why do you think the cops showed up?" I asked.

"Who knows. They must've been looking for someone. Or maybe someone complained about the crime in the area, and they decided to do a drive-by for some felon fishing, see what they could toss in the bucket," she answered, wincing.

"Well, they fucking hit the jackpot tonight." I swung my gaze to Dylan. "I killed that guy."

Dylan's one-word answer was everything. "Good."

No remorse, no second-thoughts — just clear judgment.

But it wasn't all good. "I left the gun behind."

That caused Dylan to roll her gaze my way, a scowl forming on her face. "You did what?"

"I was kinda distracted by the motherfucker beating the shit out of me and trying to rape me," I retorted. "Sorry." A sigh rattled out of Dylan as she processed the situation. I suggested lamely, "Maybe we could go back...it might still be there. I mean, it was dark and everyone was running away. It could still be where I dropped it."

"It's gone, or the cops have it," Dylan said, shaking her head. "This could be bad. Best case scenario, some thug picked it up before the cops could snag it but not likely. That gun is part of a murder investigation now. And your fucking prints are all over it. Jesus, Nic..."

I had a thousand caustic responses waiting on my

tongue, but she was right. I screwed up. I didn't have the luxury of rookie screw-ups. All they had to do was run forensics on that gun, and my record would pop right up like daisies in a field.

"We have to tell Kerri what happened," I said.

Dylan hated that idea, but what other choice did we have? *None.*

She nodded, scooting up in the seat and biting back a cry as she shifted her weight. I wiped at the blood, stinging my eye, and moved closer to her to take a look. Her throat looked ravaged. There was no mistaking the handprints on her skin. "Does it hurt to swallow?" I asked.

She nodded but said, "I'll be okay. Just need to lay low a few days. It's not the first time a mother-fucker has tried to choke me out and failed."

My weak smile in response was all I could muster. "Do you think Badger will give us hazard pay?" I asked, half-joking, half-not.

Dylan's short, derisive chuckle told me no. We were on our own. Badger didn't get bogged down with details. He wanted results. At least we delivered the package without a hitch. I guess we could put that in the win column.

But then I had to kill a man so that definitely went in the 'oh shit' column.

*Yeah, about that...*I felt nothing for the life I'd taken. Was that normal? Fuck no, it wasn't. It seemed since the auction, everything I did was simply an act of self-preservation. I didn't have time to question the morality of my actions.

I was chipping away at a fundamental part of myself that was essential for everyday human life. There was no turning back after the things I'd seen and done.

Kerri had asked, 'What's after?' and the answer seemed all the more apparent.

There was no after.

I couldn't see a future beyond a day or two ahead. Was that a protection mechanism for myself? I couldn't stress about a future I wasn't going to have if I never thought that far?

I risked another glance at Dylan. Her head rested on hard plastic, eyes closed, breathing shallowly against the onslaught of pain.

Something told me she never worried about tomorrow. Today was grim enough. Every day was a struggle for people like Dylan. I never understood the truth behind the sentiment that someone out there always had it worse because my life had been such a shit-show.

I understood now.

The entire time I'd been fixated on getting away from Carla and her shitty decisions as a mother, I never took the time to appreciate the little blessings in my life.

For all her shortcomings (and there were plenty) Carla had made sure we had someplace to live, we had *some* food to eat and that I went to school every day (even if she did go out of her way to make sure I didn't enjoy any measure of success.)

Dylan hadn't seen the inside of a classroom since she was eleven years old. What was that? Sixth grade? Maybe fifth? Her gaps in education showed in her speech sometimes, but she was smarter than anyone I knew. If given half the chance, Dylan would've been something.

I blinked away stupid tears. Was I crying for myself, for Dylan, or for every kid whose future got cut short by circumstances out of their control? I didn't know. My head was throbbing, and I wanted to throw up. It wasn't like I had a real handle on my situation right now.

All I knew was that I'd come close to dying tonight.

Dylan, too.

And yet, we'd limped away.

We were like alley cats, slipping past death in

one narrow escape after another, using up those nine lives like there's no end to the second chances.

But I knew better. Our luck would run out at some point.

If we didn't start getting workable leads, Madame Moirai wouldn't have to worry about us mucking up her operation because we'd be in the ground somewhere, and nothing would change for those deviant fuckers.

Now *that* made me want to cry.

Not tears of self-pity, sadness, or even fear but tears of frustration and rage.

I'm talking about the kind of violent, uncontrollable emotion that burned bridges and ruined lives.

I hated the idea that she might skate without consequence.

I had to find a way to stop all of them.

I sniffed back blood and snot as the train lurched to a stop with a familiar squeal. I roused Dylan with a murmured, "Time to go."

We pulled our hoodies more securely around our faces and exited the subway car to hustle to the apartment.

We made it inside, climbing through the bedroom window like usual, relieved to be somewhere safe when we were blinded by the sudden flood of light as someone flipped the switch.

One lucky guess as to who was standing there, scowling like a bear and looking like he wanted to finish us off as he barked, "What the fuck kind of trouble have you gotten yourself into this time?"

Yeah, Hicks.

Of all the times for him to wake up from a drunken stupor only to discover we'd bailed, it had to be this night.

Things just kept getting better.

8

Dylan and I exchanged looks that said, "So, how do we play this?" but Hicks didn't give us a chance to start spinning a story.

"Get your busted asses in here," he said, surveying the damage. "You don't look so good. Are you okay?"

"That's a loaded question," I answered, sinking onto the bed gingerly as Dylan wobbled past me to the bathroom. "My head feels like it's about to pop off, and I think I might have a concussion, but I'm alive."

"Same," Dylan called out from the toilet, then muttered, "Fuck, pissing blood again."

Hicks compressed his lips in a tight line, grabbing his cell to place a terse call to Kerri. "Yeah, I know it's late. I need you here. Come quick — and bring a medkit if you've got one."

"What happened?"

"We got jumped," I answered.

"By Avalon people?" he asked.

I shook my head. "Just fucking felons from the wrong gang. We were running a job for Badger."

"Goddamn it, I fucking knew you two were still running for him. What the fuck is wrong with you? You think it's safe for you to be running around acting like baby gangsters when there's a huge price on your little heads?"

Hicks was pissed. Probably the most pissed I'd ever seen him. He looked ready to punch holes in the wall, but I wasn't afraid of violence from Hicks. If anything, his reaction had the opposite effect. I knew he cared.

Dylan wobbled from the bathroom and sat next to me. Hicks saw the marks on her neck and gestured with a dark scowl, asking for details. "How'd that happen?"

"Fucker tried to choke me out before raping me. Guess he didn't like girls who move around too much."

The sarcasm in her tone hit a tender spot. My eyes welled. We were both almost raped. *Again.*

It was all too similar to what'd happened to us with our buyers. Sure, the surroundings were different, but the men were the same. "Let me take a look," he said gruffly. For all his growl, he was gentle when he touched Dylan. "Your voice is a little hoarse. Probably bruised your vocal cords. Try not to use your voice too much. Let Nicole do the talking."

Dylan didn't argue and nodded. At that moment, she was simply a girl needing someone else to take over, even if only temporarily, because she was in pain and vulnerable.

He looked to me, realizing I was holding my side. "Let me see."

I hesitated but slowly lifted the hem of my shirt to reveal the ugly bruising already blooming across my skin from taking a boot to the ribs. "It might be broken," I admitted.

Hicks agreed, muttering, "Sonofabitch," before abruptly leaving the room and returning with his Jack Daniels and some ibuprofen. "Here, take these and wash it down with this. It'll help with the pain."

I accepted the bottle, tossed back the pain killer, and swigged the bottle, nearly gagging but finally got it down. The whiskey burned my throat, but the warmth was soothing.

Dylan smirked as she took a drink, saying,

"Seems like old times. My old man used to give me a shot of whiskey after he'd walloped me good. It always helped me to forget that I'd just gotten the shit kicked out of me." She lifted the bottle with a derisive grin. "Cheers."

"You zip it. Save your vocal cords," Hicks said. To me, he said, "We can wrap your ribs. There's not much else that can be done for busted ribs as long as you don't feel anything poking your lungs. You can breathe, right?"

"Yeah, just hurts."

Hicks understood. "Busted rib sucks, but it'll heal."

It wasn't long before Kerri showed up, concern in her eyes, and medkit in her hands.

"Jesus," she breathed in horror when she got an eyeful of our battle wounds. "What the hell happened?"

"Wrong place, wrong time," I answered. Kerri shot me a look that said she'd need more details after she was done cleaning and bandaging our wounds, and we didn't argue.

When she was done, Dylan was already starting to nod off and crawled into the bed, asleep in seconds.

Kerri agreed that I had a mild concussion and

wouldn't let me sleep until she was sure I wasn't going to die from a brain aneurysm. We left the bedroom and went into the living room where I eased myself onto the sofa.

Hicks dropped into his ratty office chair behind his desk and ignored Kerri's pointed look when he poured himself a drink.

"Okay, so what really happened?" Kerri asked.

"A job with Badger went bad," I answered sheepishly. "Like...real bad."

Kerri pursed her lips. "I won't say I told you so but, the proof is in the pudding."

I smiled, grateful for the small favor.

"But what you did...was really stupid."

My smile faded. "It gets worse," I admitted.

"How could it be worse?" Kerri asked, her brow knitting.

I bit my lip. The words were stuck in my mouth. I swallowed, saying, "I killed someone tonight..." Kerri's eyes widened, but before she could say anything, I added, "And I left the gun at the crime scene."

Kerri stared, processing. I saw the detective in her warring against the adult who cared about a scared kid on the run.

Hicks chuckled, even though there was nothing

funny about this situation and lifted his bottle. "You sure you don't want that shot?"

"For fuck's sake," she muttered, rubbing her brow. "Okay, walk me through the details."

"There isn't much more to tell. We were attacked. One of King's men recognized Dylan as one of Badger's crew. Apparently, there's some kind of turf war between criminal dirtbags. We tried to leave, but they wouldn't let us. Badger gave me a gun for protection. I pulled the gun, mostly to get them to back off and leave us alone. He called my bluff and grabbed me. The gun went off, and he was dead."

"You're sure he was dead?"

"Well, he had a pretty good-sized hole in his chest, and he wasn't breathing," I answered with a small shrug. "Seemed pretty dead to me."

"Okay. So it was self-defense. At least there's that small detail working in your favor."

Hicks poured himself another drink. "Not exactly," he disagreed with a sardonic grin. "It's not like you can report it. The minute she goes into the system, even as a vic, those fuckers are going to come running. If anything, this situation works in their favor, not ours."

"I know that," Kerri grumbled. "But if anyone picked up that gun and runs prints..."

"Her DNA is going to be all over it, and she's going to pop up in the system. See? This is why you should drink."

But Kerri was already thinking of solutions. "I have to get ahead of this. First thing in the morning, I'll poke around and see who was on shift last night in Vice. Hopefully, it was one of the lazier fuckers, and the gun was missed. With any luck, some other D-bag picked up the gun and ran off with it before the cops could grab it."

"I was hoping that, too. Dylan didn't think that was likely."

"It's probably not," Kerri agreed grimly. "But maybe we'll catch a break."

"I'm sorry for screwing things up," I said, pursing my lips against the pain. "I didn't realize how bad things could go sidewise."

Kerri seemed to understand how big my admission was and pulled me gently to her. I leaned against her shoulder, tears not far behind. "It's okay. We'll figure it out. In the meantime, please promise me that you're not going to run with Badger anymore."

I nodded, sniffing back tears. "It's not easy for me to ask for help," I said. "It just seemed like I was being a mooch when I could do something for easy cash."

"Doesn't feel so easy now, does it?" Kerri admonished gently.

I shook my head. "Not so much."

Hicks yawned, the fatigue and general abuse of his body showing in the haggard puffiness of his face. "Not much more we can do about it tonight. I'm hitting the bed. You staying?" he asked Kerri.

"If you don't mind...I want to keep an eye on the girls for the night."

"Fine by me. I'm not much of a nurse." Hicks rose on stiff legs and disappeared behind his bedroom door.

"He seems like he doesn't care, but he does," Kerri said.

"I know."

Kerri chuckled, pushing a lock of hair away from my eyes, reminding me gently not to sleep when my eyes started to flutter shut. "A concussion is a serious injury. I need you to stay awake a little while longer."

"I'm so tired," I complained, feeling like a little kid.

"I know. Just a little while longer."

I sighed, unhappy, but tried to stay awake. "Tell me we're going to beat them," I said.

She knew I was talking about The Avalon network.

"We're going to try like hell," she answered, not willing to lie. I smiled, oddly comforted. I preferred an ugly truth to a pretty lie.

"My rib hurts like a bitch," I murmured, wincing when I tried shifting to a different position. "Like really bad."

"You both needed a hospital," Kerri said, worried.

"Probably."

"Do you think you'd recognize any of the people who attacked you and Dylan?" she asked.

I closed my eyes, but my mind was a chaotic jumble. All I could manage was an overall feeling of panic and the need to survive. I shook my head. "Sorry, probably not." I didn't want to. I had enough monsters in my head.

"It's okay." She laid her head gently against the crown of mine. "Kid, you've been through enough to last two lifetimes. I'm sorry. You deserve better."

"We all do," I said.

I meant that for her, too. "I'm sorry we're making a mess of your life. Before we came around, you probably had a lot less stress."

"That might be true, but I'm glad you're in my life. You and Dylan are special kids."

Kerri smelled faintly of leather and citrus, something masculine, but somehow on her, it smelled like safety and warmth. I closed my eyes, releasing a pent-up breath. "You would've liked Jilly," I said. "She was sweet. Not like Dylan and me. Her middle name was Jewell. Can you believe that? Crazy, huh? It was kinda perfect for her."

"I wish I could've met her," Kerri said.

"Yeah. She would've liked you, too. I think Jilly liked everyone if they were nice to her. Probably a mistake in this world, but it made her pretty special."

Why was I babbling about Jilly? I didn't know. I switched tracks. "Do you believe in God?"

"I want to, but when you've seen as much as I have...faith is hard to hold onto. I really want to believe that there's something or someone driving the bus. I guess it gives me comfort when I've got nothing left."

My eyelids dragged. I wished I could believe in something. My faith in anyone or anything was a vast wasteland of nothing.

But like Kerri, I guess I wanted to believe that if there was a God, there was a heaven and a hell, too. I wanted Jilly floating on clouds, eating goodness, and burping rainbows. I wanted Tana doing whatever made Tana giggle and smile.

And I wanted everyone who'd ever associated with Madame Moirai to die a horrible death, then wake up in hell where the devil painted the walls with their guts, over and over.

That made me smile.

But it didn't help the ever-widening chasm swallowing up my soul and obliterating everything about myself I'd once held dear.

I guess that was the cost of survival.

And why fate knew some — like Jilly and Tana — simply couldn't pay the bill.

9

It takes more than a few days to heal a broken rib, but that's all I had available. Chances like the fundraiser weren't dropping from trees, so I had no choice but to suck it up and move forward with the original plan.

Hicks came through with a confirmed guest list, and while I didn't recognize any names, we'd used our time sitting on the couch by combing through the Internet, trying to match names to faces. Our hope was that we'd get lucky and either Dylan or I would recognize someone from the auction.

Just when I thought Lady Luck had officially put us on the black-ball list, she decided to throw us a bone.

"Holy fucking shit...it's him," I hissed with revulsion, staring at the foreign name but the face that was burned into my brain.

I gestured wildly at the screen as both Dylan and Hicks crowded in for a better look.

Dylan peered at the screen. "Is that your buyer?" she asked.

I nodded, my cheeks heating as I stared at his hatefully handsome face. No, check that, *not* handsome...I saw past the cut jaw and expensive grooming. I saw a monster.

Hicks' lip curled. "He looks like the kind of fucker who'd buy a kid for sex. They all have a vibe about them. I've seen a few one too many times when I was a cop. Fuckers all deserve a hot poker up the ass."

"No argument here," I murmured, unable to drag my gaze away from the screen. "He told me his name was Henri Benoit...I can't believe I actually believed that was his name."

Hicks grabbed a notebook and pencil. "Well, Mr. Franklin Dubois better pucker up his pie hole because we're gonna bring the hurt," he said with a note of glee in his tone that I'd never heard before, but I liked it. "Feeling ready to crash a party, girls?"

"Damn straight." I grinned, forgetting that my side still hurt like a bitch, and my bruises told a story without a happy ending. I wouldn't miss this party for the world. "Maybe our luck is finally changing."

Dylan didn't seem as excited. "What if he recognizes you?" she queried sharply. "If you remember him, he's likely to remember you. Especially when Madame Moirai probably sent out a text message or something saying that you were on the loose. You're the only one he offered to elevate. He's going to remember you."

I didn't want to believe that, but a little seed of doubt had sprouted against my wishes. "Even if he does remember me, I doubt Madame Moirai said anything. She's not likely to do anything that would spook her rich clientele. As far as she's concerned, we're just inconvenient loose ends that will eventually get snipped. I'm probably the last thing on his mind."

"Rich people don't like it when someone tells them no. It becomes personal. You're delusional if you don't believe that fucker thinks about you every night. The rest of us were disposable. You were the only one worth keeping. Remember that."

I hated Dylan's assessment for multiple reasons. One, I hated that the buyers didn't give a second thought as to what happened to the girls after they'd been used and abused. Two, I really hated the idea that Henri or whatever the fuck his name was, would think about me at all.

"Dylan might be right," Hicks said, frowning. "But we'll have to take the risk. We're not going to get another chance at some serious intel without this fundraiser."

A tiny tremor rattled my spine as my mouth dried. What would I do if Henri — sorry, *Franklin* — recognized me? What would he do? I looked to Dylan for reassurance.

Dylan was quick to remind me, "Kerri will make sure nothing happens to us."

Kerri managed to snag a security position for the night. According to Kerri, it wasn't all that uncommon for off-duty cops to provide event security for extra cash.

Her reminder lessened my sudden anxiety. I had zero doubt that Kerri would rip anyone apart who threatened us. I nodded. "You're right. It'll be fine. Although, I wouldn't mind watching Kerri back Franklin into a corner and work him over with a nightstick or something. Maybe even a Taser? That'd be cool to watch him squirm and shit himself in his fancy clothes."

"Savage," Dylan said with approval. "Can't say I'd hate that either."

Hicks chuckled. "All right, you blood-thirsty heathens, I've got credentials for you as servers, and you're to report to the kitchen area at 4 p.m. Wear your wigs, just to be safe."

"I've been wearing this wig for so long I'm starting to identify as a brunette," I quipped with a smart-ass grin. "And all this time I was told blondes have more fun."

Dylan, a natural brunette, chuckled but disagreed. "Naw, you're better as a dirty blonde. Suits your face. You've got that California girl thing going on."

"Hey, I only spent a short time in California. I'm a New Yorker through and through and don't you forget it."

We joked a little more and then started to get ready for our big night.

Hicks had connections all over this city. In addition to getting the confirmed guest list, he secured credentials from the catering company working at the event. I didn't ask for details because all that mattered was that we were in.

Dylan and I spent a lot of time fixing our faces to hide the bruises, and Dylan helped wrap my ribs so I could move without collapsing in pain. I couldn't risk being loopy, so I eschewed the pain killer for a handful of ibuprofen and hoped for the best.

Dressed in crisp white uniforms with our credentials pinned to our chest, we slipped through the back door to the kitchen like we belonged there, and no one seemed to notice.

The kitchen teemed with activity as servers, line cooks, and the chef bustled around the gleaming stainless steel preparing rich people food, starting with the hors-d'oeuvres.

A terse, harried line cook shoved a tray of something disgusting in our hands and gestured for us to start circulating, saying in a sharp tone, "Go! Make yourself useful!" and we were shoved out the double doors into the glitzy hall.

I glanced down at the goo on the cracker and grimaced with disgust. "Rich people eat weird shit," I said beneath my breath.

"Looks like a pigeon came along and shit on this cracker," Dylan said with the same expression. "I think that's...fish eggs or something? I've eaten out of garbage cans with more appealing food than this."

Throngs of posh people circulated in the room, dressed as if they were meeting the Queen of England as light, classical music spread from the live band on the raised dais. I pasted a fake smile on my face and murmured, "It's go time," as we entered the den of lions, in the hopes of finding a snake.

My nerves were strung tight, but I covered my anxiety with polite smiles as I circulated through the room, playing the part.

"Thank you, darling," one woman said, selecting a cracker with zeal. Her eyes lit up with delight as she savored the tidbit of terrible trash. "Ohh, exquisite. Divine! I must have another..."

I smiled and waited for her to make a selection, then moved away, internally shaking my head. If I lived to be a hundred (which wasn't likely), I'd never understand rich people.

A stately woman with stiffly coiffed blonde hair held court with fawning people all around her. She was probably in her mid-50s, but it was hard to tell with all the work she'd had done to her face. Botox to smooth the lines, fillers to plump up the cheeks and lips, and possibly an eye lift to get rid of any natural sagging, she could've been 80 years old for all I knew.

But she had a presence about her, that was for sure. She wore a simple black dress, classy and understated, yet she vibrated with influence. No wonder everyone was flocked around her like a bunch of bees looking for pollen.

"How much you want to bet, that's the Head of Social Services," I said, nudging Dylan.

"Well, she's definitely popular. Everyone wants to rub elbows with her."

"I want to get a closer look," I said. "Chances are the snakes are going to want to be as close as possible to the star of the event."

"Good point," Dylan agreed, following my lead.

As I worked my way closer, I kept a sharp eye on the crowd, looking for anyone who might trigger recognition but also staying wary of Franklin popping up.

When I didn't see anyone I recognized, I felt safe enough to approach her.

"Hors d'oeuvres?" I offered, lifting the plate for her perusal.

The woman graciously declined, saying, "Oh goodness, I never really acquired a taste for caviar, but thank you."

One point in her favor for having tastebuds.

"Me either," I said with a small smile, waiting for the others to finish mauling the plate. "But to each his own."

"Indeed." She paused a minute, then said, "You have lovely eyes."

"Thank you," I murmured, surprised she was

taking the time to talk to me when there were plenty of people trying to get her attention. "So do you."

She acknowledged my awkward compliment with a nod, and I excused myself with the valid excuse that I needed to refill my platter.

Dylan met me in the hallway. "What was that about?"

"She just started talking to me. I couldn't be rude that would've been noticed."

"Yeah, but she seemed to take an interest in you that was weird."

"She was just being nice, setting a good example. I'm sure it's all an act for the people around her."

"Yeah, that makes sense. Everyone in this place is fake as fuck."

"There's enough plastic to start a Barbie factory," I quipped, earning a snicker from Dylan. "But so far, I don't see anyone that I recognize. Do you?"

"Not yet, but the evening just started. People are still arriving. That whole 'fashionably late' thing is all the rage for rich people, I hear."

I agreed. "Guess I'd better get another tray of pigeon poop before the masses get too hungry."

"I wonder what the main course is going to be?" Dylan asked with a curled lip.

"Probably stewed monkey or something equally disgusting."

"People eat monkeys? For real?" Dylan looked at me in horror.

I shrugged. "I don't know. Maybe. Probably. I mean, who looks at a fish egg and says, I bet that would taste really good on a cracker'?"

"For real."

We disappeared behind the double doors, received fresh platters, and then sent back out.

So far, it'd been smooth sailing but empty waters. I didn't know if I was disappointed or relieved that I hadn't seen Franklin among the hoity-toity, self-important assholes.

I wasn't even sure what I would do if I did see him.

A bunch of scenarios played in my head, such as throwing the platter in his face and kicking him in the nuts or kicking him in the nuts and pushing him down a flight of stairs. In my darkest scenario, I simply shot him, watching without emotion as he bled out and died.

Except I didn't have a gun anymore, so that scenario was unlikely.

So, I had to make do with what I had available — a platter and my foot.

Not as satisfying, but at least it was something. I grinned to myself at the idea of crushing his testicles with an Olympic soccer level kick to the groin. I could almost hear him howl. Now *that* was something worth imagining.

The funny thing about real-life scenarios...they never turned out the way you imagine.

Sometimes you're not the bad-ass in the story.

Sometimes you're just a scared kid facing down the boogeyman with nothing but a plate of useless crackers.

Paralyzed with fear.

"Hello...*Nee-cole...*"

And backed into a corner.

10

My skin prickled. I knew that voice. There was no mistaking the way he pronounced my name with a subtle French flair, the way he drew out the vowels and softened the consonants, drawing out the pronunciation until it sounded like something exotic and unique.

God, how I hated it.

I slowly turned, my fingers gripping the platter as my palms became slick. I lifted my gaze and held his narrowed stare. "hors d'oeuvre?" I asked, pretending I didn't recognize him.

The cruel twist of his mouth reminded me of that night. "You are of a mind to play games?" he surmised, stepping toward me. My gaze darted, looking for help, but somehow I'd ended up in a darkened corner, away from the throng of people. "As you recall, I too enjoy games."

I wasn't ready to face him. I tried to pretend I was confused by his statement. "I'm sorry, you must have me confused for someone else. My name isn't Nicole."

"The hair is different, but a cheap wig is no disguise," he said, tsking at my attempt at subterfuge. "I would remember your face...your body anywhere."

A flush swept across my skin as revulsion twisted my gut. "Excuse me...I have to get back to work," I said, trying to move past him but he grabbed my arm and pulled me close. I nearly gagged at the smell of his cologne as memories blotted out every rational thought. I growled, "Let me go."

"You belong to me, sweet Nicole," he said, bending to whisper in my ear. "Have you forgotten you were bought and paid for? I own your flesh. I've missed having you in my bed. You will leave with me tonight."

The fuck I will.

"If you don't let me go, I will start screaming my head off," I promised with a hiss. "Let's see how quickly your rich friends abandon you when they find out what a sick fuck you are."

His grip tightened on my arm. I could feel the finger bruises forming. "You have been a naughty girl, haven't you? Causing all sorts of problems. I knew you were something special the moment I saw you on the block. I would've paid double for you that night. You were worth every cent, but now, you've become a liability. Do you understand that? The price on your pretty head is quite high. How much is your life worth, Nicole? I can protect you from what is coming."

"*You* protect *me*? That's fucking bold. I know all about what happens to auction girls after you're done with them. How much blood is on your hands, you sick bastard? How many girls have you ruined?"

He jerked me close, nuzzling my neck as if we weren't in danger of being seen at any minute. I cringed, loathing the press of his lips against my skin. Tears sprung to my eyes, and the platter in my hands started to shake. "What is pleasure without pain?"

"I don't know, you tell me," I said right before I drove my elbow straight into his gut, sending crackers flying. He grunted, doubling over from the unexpected hit, giving me the chance to bolt, but before I got two steps away, his hand snatched at my wig, ripping it from my head.

I tried to scream, but his arm snaked around and

cut off my windpipe, nearly mashing my vocal cords. I kicked in terror as he dragged me deeper into an isolated area, his free hand cruelly crushing my breast, causing tears to spring to my eyes.

"I've missed you. Your fire is worth every inconvenience," he said, his tone hardening. "I look forward to breaking you all over again."

He was dragging me out of the room toward a side door in the building. If he managed to get me outside, I wouldn't escape. He'd have me at his mercy. I couldn't let that happen.

I would die before I let him touch me ever again. He let go of my breast long enough to open the door, and it gave me a split second to react. I squirmed like a spoiled toddler, sliding down his body to reach down and grab his nuts, twisting as hard as he'd abused my tit.

He sucked in a wild gasp as I nearly ripped his balls off. Franklin dropped to his knees, his eyes rolling back in his head as he cradled his nuts. "You never fucking broke me, you sack of shit, but I promise, I *will* break you." I snatched my wig from the floor and ran, but he was hot on my tail.

I weaved my way through the crowd, wiping at the tears in my eyes and ignoring the stunned looks of people as I pushed past them. I was half-blind from my panic, and the driving need to get the hell away from Franklin that I ran smack into Bitsy Aldridge, and nearly sent the belle of the ball straight to the floor.

"Oof!" The woman grunted as I barreled into her, but she caught us both before we tumbled to the floor. I mumbled an apology and tried to push past her, but her grip was strong as she held me in place. "Hold on, are you okay?" she asked, concerned. "Why are you running?"

I glanced backward and saw Franklin stop short and retreat into the shadows when he saw me with Bitsy. My heart thundered in my chest, making it hard to catch my breath. I wanted to rat the bastard out. I wanted to scream to everyone in this fancy place that they were rubbing elbows with a fucking murderer, but the timing wasn't right. I swallowed and tried to slow my breathing, finally saying, "I'm sorry...I have a family emergency. I have to go."

"Oh dear, well, let's get you home. I'll have my staff speak to your supervisor and make sure you get a full night's wage."

I peered at her in surprise. I wasn't expecting kindness from someone who traveled in these circles. But seeing as I wasn't actually on the payroll, her offer might create bigger problems. "Oh, that's okay, you don't have to do that."

"Of course I do. This is New York. The cost of living is ridiculously high. Unless you're independently wealthy, I'm sure losing out on a night's wage is a serious situation in your budget."

Budget. Ha! I wish I had the problem of managing a budget. Staying alive was my main concern. I smiled and pretended to see someone I knew. "Oh! There's my ride. I'm so sorry. Best of luck with your fundraiser. I hope you raise lots of cash."

I pulled away just as she was asking my name and kept moving. I didn't dare look back. I'd already made a scene. My cover was blown. I had to find Dylan and Kerri.

Dylan was sneaking a few bites of food from the plates before she carried them out. I grabbed her, my eyes wild. "Franklin found me. He almost dragged me out of the building!"

"Holy shit! Are you okay? Jesus, where is he now? How'd you get away?"

"I don't have time to explain. We have to go. He ripped my wig off!" I held up my wig and shook it for emphasis. "And he fucking nearly crushed my tit to death. He recognized me right away. Even with the wig."

Dylan's expression darkened, popping something in her mouth, and chewing quickly. "I told you he'd never forget about you. Shit, now he knows you're still alive and in the city."

"Exactly. Which is why we have to go now."

Dylan nodded. "Text Kerri, and let her know we're bailing."

We snuck out the back, but not before Dylan grabbed a whole plate of miniature eclairs that were supposed to be for dessert and shoved them in a plastic bag.

When I stared with incredulous disbelief, she said, "What? Have you ever had one of these little cakes? They're incredible! Seriously, rich people might eat weird shit, but they get the best stuff, too."

I shook my head and motioned for her to hurry up. We scuttled out the back and ran from the building to disappear down the subway tunnel. We caught the train and dropped into the hard chairs, breathing hard.

Before we'd even caught our breath, Dylan reached into her bag and stuffed a small pastry in her mouth, groaning. "Goddamn, this is so good. Here, try one. It'll make everything better."

I crooked a small smile and accepted. Funny, Lora had always believed anything could be solved with a fresh pastry. My mind was still racing, but I took a bite.

"It's good, right?" Dylan asked, looking for validation or maybe, some indication I wasn't about to collapse into a sobbing mess.

"Yeah, pretty good."

We chewed in silence. I wasn't sure if tonight had been a success or not. Franklin knew I was alive. He'd likely tell Madame Moirai. Seeing him again had made me sick to my stomach.

The realization that he still had some kind of power over me made me feel worse.

"I froze," I admitted. Dylan looked at me in question, working on her second eclair. I glanced down at my own unfinished pastry. "In the moment, I froze."

"How did you think you'd react?"

"I don't know...more bad-ass? More confident... just more of something. Or maybe less of what I actually did."

She wiped her mouth, understanding. "Yeah, I get it. In my mind, I like to think that if I saw my buyer, I'd rip his guts out with my bare hands but who knows? Maybe I'd react the same way. Probably. I was really nervous that I might see him at the fundraiser. I nearly shit myself twice when I thought I saw him."

"Yeah?" Dylan had never given any indication she was anything but hard as stone. Her confession made me feel better about myself. "But he wasn't there, right?"

"Not that I could see. I guess all rich folk don't party together like we'd hoped."

"Well, Franklin was there. The fucker thought he could drag me out of the building like he was my master or something. He said he owned me."

"Those fuckers got balls of steel," Dylan said with a glower.

I grinned. "Yeah, but I 'bout twisted those balls right off. He's gonna be thinking about me for the next couple days as he ices his nuts."

Dylan cackled with amusement. "Damn straight. That's dope as hell, girl. Let's hope for an infection or something to sweeten the retribution a little."

We bumped fists. "Sounds good to me."

But I didn't understand how I could kill a man one minute and the next, freeze like a little baby in the next. I sighed, stuffing the last of the eclair in my mouth.

Somehow Dylan knew what I was thinking.

"You're too hard on yourself. The way trauma

sits on the brain is never equal, and it never plays by the rules. I thought I wouldn't give two shits about my dad, and if given a chance, I'd end him. But that's not how I reacted at all."

I looked at her sharply. "What do you mean?"

Dylan took a minute to wipe the corners of her mouth before sharing, "I saw him once. I think I was fifteen? I'd already hooked up with Badger's crew, and I was running a job. I saw him in a liquor store — big surprise — and I literally couldn't move. I froze like a rabbit. He never saw me, just kept on walking, oblivious to the kid staring at him from across the street."

"Damn," I murmured, shaking my head. "What happened after that?"

"Nothing. *Absolutely* nothing. I stood there watching him until he turned the corner and then he was gone again. I felt sick to my stomach because I didn't do anything. I didn't even cuss him out for being the low-life loser, deadbeat dad that he was. I just...watched him walk away — and I haven't seen him since."

I digested Dylan's admission. I knew the hatred she had for her father. Yet, she'd reacted in the same way as me. Maybe human beings were programmed the same. I peeped another glance at Dylan. "Do you still regret not doing anything?"

She shrugged. "Not really. He's part of my past, you know? And that's where I'm leaving him."

I nodded. "Makes sense. If he's not going to be part of your future...no sense in dragging him along with you."

"Exactly."

"I still wish I'd done something more than go catatonic," I said in a small voice. "I wish I'd had Badger's gun. I think I would've shot him."

"Maybe. Maybe not. Hard to say."

Dylan never failed to surprise me. Just when I thought she was two-dimensional, she laid some serious wisdom that left my head spinning.

Dylan reached for one last eclair but stopped with a groan, gripping her stomach. "I think I hit my limit."

I chuckled with knowing, looking forward. "Yeah...me too."

11

Kerri paced the small apartment, making it feel ten times smaller than it actually was. "This happened right beneath my nose. I can't believe he dared to put his hands on you in plain view of all those people," she said, heated. I knew she was beating herself up, but it wasn't her fault, it was mine for not paying attention to my surroundings.

"It wasn't exactly in plain view. I was fucking around and wandered off. He found me in a darkened alcove. I was taking a breather, and the next thing I knew, he'd grabbed me. It happened super fast. I barely had time to react."

"He was probably watching you. He must've recognized you way before you ever saw him. He followed you into that alcove with a plan," Kerri said, her gaze darkening.

I hadn't thought of that possibility, but it made sense. The fucker had totally stalked me. If it weren't for Bitsy Aldridge, he might've caught me. "When he saw her talking to me, he backed off."

Kerri nodded, deep in thought. She looked at Hicks. "So the girls didn't recognize anyone but Nicole's buyer Franklin Dubois at the event, but now that we have a real name, we can start running him down."

"Already on it," Hicks said. "While you guys were rubbing elbows with the one percent, I was poking around in his business."

I perked up. "Did you find anything?"

"I got an address here in New York," Hicks said.

A hungry grin formed on Dylan's lips as she said, "What are we waiting for? Let's pay him a midnight visit."

"Hold up, this isn't going to be an assassination," Kerri warned. "We need hard evidence to put these people away. We also need proof that Dubois is connected to The Avalon, or else we're just wasting our time. They've likely got a stable of shark lawyers just waiting to shoot down anything that isn't irrefutable."

"Who are we kidding? Nothing we throw at them is going to stick, no matter what kind of hard evidence we throw at them," Dylan scoffed, irritated at being denied. "How else do you think they've managed to skate past any charges or consequences all these years? I say we go old-school, cap the motherfuckers and call it a day. Maybe it'll send a message that they better watch their backs because we're coming for them."

I shrugged. "Sounds good to me." I liked the idea of putting a bullet in Franklin's smug face. "Dylan's right. We're kidding ourselves if we think we're going to be able to catch them with the long arm of justice."

Hicks didn't disagree, but he didn't back us up either. I think he didn't want to piss Kerri off, so he remained silent.

Kerri sighed and said, "Girls, we have to try. If I let you guys go in there vigilante-style, ...we're no better than they are."

"That's your problem, Kerri...you're so busy worrying about being better than they are, but honestly, we just want to see them dead. We don't care about rising above. We want payback."

"Don't you want a life after this is all done?" Kerri shot back with exasperation. "If you kill any of the people connected to the Madame, you're going to go to prison, and *they* win. Don't you see that? Think bigger, Dylan. Think beyond this moment. Try to think about the future."

Kerri was wasting her breath, trying to preach to Dylan. That girl hadn't thought of a future since she left home. She lived every moment as if it were her last because it could be. Looking forward was a luxury reserved for those who didn't have to pay with their body and soul.

Dylan's voice hardened. "What I want is every fucker whoever paid into the auction to know true fear right before they die. If I can be the one who delivers, even better. That's what I want, and no one, not even you, can make me feel bad about it."

Kerri and Dylan faced off. We were putting Kerri in a bad position. It was her job to stop criminals from doing criminal things. There was no room for vigilantes if you're following the letter of the law. It wasn't Kerri's fault that we existed somewhere in the gray.

"We won't kill Franklin," I promised when the tension was so thick you could choke on it. "But we need to see what he knows. The only way to do that is to pay him a little visit."

"Let me get a warrant."

This time Hicks interjected. "With what probable cause? No judge's going to sign off on a warrant with so little to go on. Besides, that stable of shark lawyers you mentioned would tear that flimsy warrant to shreds. C'mon Kerri, the girls are smarter than you give them credit. Don't blow smoke up their ass."

Kerri looked torn. She knew Hicks was right, but breaking the law went against the grain in Kerri's world.

She shook her head, grabbing her coat in a quick, agitated motion. "I have to go. I'll call you later," not bothering with a hollow request for us to stay put because she knew we wouldn't.

I watched Kerri leave, my heart heavy. Kerri cared about us, which was more than I could say about most adults we'd had in our lives. While having Kerri in our corner was a plus, it was also a burden. For the first time in my life, I had to think about how my actions might affect another person.

Having someone care about me, I mean, *really* care about me, tilted my axis. I couldn't afford that kind of distraction. I shook off the feelings and focused on the situation. "We need access to his place. Chances are, he's got some fancy security system, but I bet he also has a cleaning service. If we could get fake credentials as one of the cleaning services like we did for the catering company, we could walk right in."

"Not bad," Hicks said, agreeing. "I'll see what I can dig up."

"So, are we killing him?" Dylan asked without flinching. "You probably want dibs, right?"

Hicks chuckled but cut Dylan off. "Look, Kerri was right about a few things. You can't go capping people just because you want to. If that were the case, we'd all have blood on our hands from something. We need something we can work with. Dubois is a cog in the wheel. We need to know how's really in charge, who's pulling strings."

"And you think that fucker will know anything? Can we at least torture him? I think I could talk Badger into working him over for us," Dylan said.

"Not ruling that out as a possibility, but let's do our own recon first," Hicks said.

For a split second, I was outside my body, listening to us casually discuss killing or, at the very least, torturing another human being. I couldn't believe the words coming out of my own mouth. And to think, at one time, I'd really thought I was a bad-ass.

"So, we get access to his crib...what are we looking for?" I asked.

"Any paperwork or pictures would work."

I scoffed. "Like anyone keeps hard copies of anything anymore."

"For normal transactions, I'd agree," Hicks said, pausing to light a cigarette. "But digital trails are a liability in this day and age. Why do you think the FBI has such a strong kiddie porn task force? Everyone thinks they've got their shit hidden when in fact, their trail of bread crumbs is like a fucking neon sign if you know how to follow the tracks."

I hadn't thought of that. "Okay, so where should we look if he were going to hide shit?"

"Depends on the person. Some people hide their shit in plain sight, and some go to great lengths to disguise their stash. Just keep your eyes open and look for anything that seems a little off."

"That narrows it down," I retorted. "Easy for you to say, you're not the one putting your ass on the line."

Hicks' smile faded. "Look, if I could get away with doing this myself, I'd do it in a heartbeat, but something tells me, I can't pull off the cleaning service look without drawing attention to myself. It's gotta be you two, and I hate it."

I believed him. No sense in making him feel worse when he didn't have to help us at all. Hicks was a lot of things, but deep down, he was a good man.

"Cool, so get us the credentials, and we'll go super spy on the fucker," Dylan said, ready to do this. "Maybe when all this is over, I can apply for a job with the CIA or something. I think spy stuff is my jam."

I laughed, wincing as my rib protested the movement. "Settle down 007. Let's try not to get killed first before you go sending in your resume."

Dylan grinned as she sauntered to the kitchen to find some grub. "Don't be jelly, honey. It ain't my fault I've got skills that you don't."

"How long will it take to get us credentials?" I asked.

"Depending on how thorough the security is, probably a few days," Hicks answered.

"Good. That will give my body a few more days to recoup. I feel like warmed-over dog shit."

"Kinda smell like it, too," Dylan quipped, feeling quite the sassy bitch today. She popped a few bits of dry sugared cereal in her mouth and said, "Well, you guys can sit around and mold, but I got plans."

"Yeah? Like what?"

"Don't worry about it," she chastised, and I knew right away, I didn't want to know what she was doing. It probably involved Badger, and I didn't need the stress. I was still pissed at him for sending us to get our asses kicked on Diamond Lane. It was a dick move, and he was going to get an earful from me when I was confident I could do it without ending up dead.

Dylan grabbed a can of soda from the fridge and then her jacket before heading out, saying, "Don't wait up," and then she was gone.

I exhaled, shaking my head. "That girl is addicted to toxic situations," I said.

"Aren't we all?" Hicks replied with a reflective expression. "Everyone's got their favorite poison."

Maybe so. "How do you know Badger? I mean, it doesn't seem like you two would be friends or anything. Did you meet him when you were a cop?"

"That story's not fit for young ears," he answered with a regretful smile. "Better to keep certain things to ourselves. I like you, kid. Why ruin a good thing?"

I fell silent. In his own way, he was asking me to drop it. I supposed that was fair. Not everyone felt the need to share their deepest, darkest moments. Some people held those blackened memories close to the vest or buried deep. It wasn't my place to pick at whatever he wanted to stay hidden.

It did make me wonder if it had anything to do with the reason why he wasn't a cop anymore.

"I'm going to bed," I said, faking a yawn. It was a little early, but I could always use sleep. My body was one giant bruise. My head, even worse.

I was smart enough to know that the fatigue I felt was more than physical. I was weary down to my bones. The emotional toll on my reserves was nothing short of catastrophic. I didn't even know how I managed to open my eyes each day.

One thing I did know, there wasn't a night I closed my eyes that I didn't wish I'd wake up in my old, lumpy bed to the sound of my shitty mother slurring her words to discover this shitshow had been nothing but a horrible dream.

But each day I woke up, I knew it was all real.

And that made me want to close my eyes and sleep it all away.

12

While Hicks worked on getting credentials for our new career change in the cleaning services, Kerri doubled down on the research available through the police portals.

"So, I got some background on the mortuary listed on Nova's case file. Lawson and Bergstein opened in 1920 by business partners, George Lawson, and Jeremiah Bergstein and stayed local until it was sold a few times, once in the '60s and then more recently in 2006. Here's the thing, the most recent purchase has a corporate owner on the title..." She paused before adding, "Lawson and Bergstein is owned by Avalon Inc."

My mouth dropped as a sliver of hope lodged in my heart. "That's shady, right? I mean, what's a corporation need with a mortuary unless they're up to no good."

"Not necessarily. It's not uncommon for corporations to own several different businesses in an attempt to diversify their portfolio," Kerri answered with a pursed expression. "I don't want to give you false hope that it's anything other than what it seems, but it did trip some alarms in my head."

Yeah, same. I understood Kerri's word of caution, but my gut said whatever The Avalon touched was dirty. "Can we find what else Avalon Inc owns?" I asked.

"Presumably, the Secretary of State should have all the businesses listed as owned by a corporation with a home base in the listed state, but that's assuming the shareholders aren't pulling strings to hide assets, which is likely. We'd really need a forensic accountant to chase down all these kinds of leads."

"Or a hacker with a taste for digging into personal business," Dylan piped in. "I bet Hicks knows someone. Maybe his hacker buddy who got us the RSVP list can get us info on Avalon Inc."

"Anything illegally obtained is inadmissible in court," Kerri said, not loving that idea. I knew she wanted to keep everything as legal as possible for potential evidence later, but I wasn't sure we had that luxury.

"Like this is ever going to make it to court," Dylan cackled as if the idea were absurd. "You're living a pipe dream if you think this isn't going to end in an all-or-nothing hail of gunfire type of scenario."

"Let's shoot for a less-bloody-everyone-dies option," Kerri said.

Dylan shrugged as if that wasn't her problem that Kerri was delusional. "I prefer an ugly truth to a pretty lie, but that's just me."

That was an argument for a different day. I think Dylan and I had pretty much made some kind of peace with the knowledge trying to bring down The Avalon was a suicide-bomber kind of quest.

Kerri moved on, saying, "I pulled the files of the seven girls, including Nova's, that I think might be connected to the auction network. I can't take the risk of working on this at the station because my lieutenant is up my ass about wasting time on closed cases. Luckily, he's not looking to check if the case files are missing, so I was able to bring them."

She pulled the case files and placed them on the scarred kitchen table. "I couldn't sleep last night, so I spent a few hours looking for similarities, and I found a few that I don't think are coincidental, but I want fresh eyes to confirm what I see."

Dylan and I joined her at the table, interested. Kerri hesitated, regarding Dylan. "Are you sure you want to see Nova's case file? It has autopsy pictures that you may find disturbing."

"I'm fine," Dylan said, but I could tell she was hiding her pain, trying to be stoic.

"I'll take Nova's file," I volunteered, taking the file with a firm hand. Dylan didn't stop me. Kerri nodded and handed Dylan a set of different files. I opened the first folder, my stomach clenching at the sight of the dead girl. I didn't know her, but that girl on the slab could've been me if fate had turned out differently. I swallowed and refocused my attention, shelving emotions, and detaching so I could be useful.

Each of us spent a few moments in silence as we read the files, processing the information, and looking for anything that might seem connected.

As I flipped through files, I saw what Kerri was talking about. "They all state a drug overdose as their cause of death, but they're all obviously bruised up like they were beaten." I paused a minute to confirm something else. My lips thinned as I said, "And they all list the same coroner that recently kicked the bucket like the one who signed off on their cases."

Dylan nodded, confirming the same for her case files. "So I think we can safely assume that the coroner was shady as fuck and obviously on the take. Jesus, are there any decent people left in the world?"

"Kid, in my experience, if you stay in this job too long, you lose all faith in humanity," Kerri retorted. "Depravity, greed, thieves, liars...I swear, sometimes, I think there's not a lot left of anything good to save, but then I run across kids like you — survivors — and I know there's a reason to keep trying to make the world a better place."

Both Dylan and I didn't know what to say. I think it was safe to say neither of us had ever been anyone's reason to care, and it hit us both in a deep place.

Of course, it was Dylan who broke the heavy silence first. "Yeah, well, don't go building a statue in our honor yet. I'm sure one or both of us will disappoint you soon enough."

It was meant as a dark joke, but it plucked at a genuine fear in my head. I'd spent my life feeling like a disappointment. For once, there was someone in my corner who truly cared about me, and I didn't want to fuck it up, but I probably would.

That's the thing about damaged people, they always managed to reach for the lowest bar even if they didn't want to.

But Kerri smiled and said, "We'll see," before moving on. "Okay, so yes, that's what I saw, too. And yes, I think it's a fair bet that the coroner wasn't the most moral on the payroll. Unfortunately, he's already dead, so it's not like we can shake him down for answers."

"Yeah, bet if you dig a little harder, you'll find out that he didn't exactly die of natural causes, no matter what the coroner had to say."

Kerri rubbed her forehead with a small groan. "The trail of bodies this network leaves is nothing short of homicidal efficiency."

"Yeah, they're a real bunch of Olympic-level killers," I groused, hating them. "So, what now? If your boss won't let you dig into these cases, what can we do with this information?"

"Officially? Not much, but it helps us get a better idea of how they're getting away with murder."

"Well, excuse my French, but that's fucking useless," I muttered. "We need information that helps us catch them, not just build a case that looks interesting on paper and will make a good made-for-tv movie."

Kerri exhaled a short breath, saying, "Here's the thing girls, they might seem untouchable, but eventually, everyone screws up. Especially when people get cocky. These case files go back ten years, and that's just the ones I could find. I'm willing to bet there are more. These people have been operating a highly sophisticated human trafficking ring for at least a decade, and they've become overly confident that they're not going to get caught. I've seen it a million times...hubris will bring you down every time."

"Not before more girls die," I said morosely. "We need to stop them now. I can't move on with my life like nothing happened. I need to know that they're done for good."

"Which is why you girls need to quit going off-book," Kerri implored, appealing to our sense of reason. "If we want to stop them, we have to find the boss and chop the head off, not just the legs. You understand?"

"I understand, but it's not easy," I said.

Dylan agreed with a dark glower. "You don't know what we've been through."

"I can only imagine," Kerri admitted with true pain in her eyes. "I swear to you, I will do everything in my power to put them all down, but I need your help to do it."

"We're willing to help, but you're too focused on doing everything by the book, and that's not how we're going to win," I said.

Kerri regarded me with frustration, but she knew I was right. Finally, she allowed, "Fine, a *little* bending of the rules I understand but no more vigilante bullshit. Okay?"

I wasn't sure I could agree to that without lying, but I could try. I personally wanted to slit Franklin's throat, but at this point, he was our best lead, and I couldn't fuck that up for the sake of vengeance.

I shared a look with Dylan before nodding. We didn't specify what we agreed to. We both knew that if push came to shove, we'd do what we had to, but Kerri was our best ally, and we didn't want to ruin what we had.

I double-checked something against the files in my hand, confirming another detail. "All of these girls were buried using Lawson and Bergstein Mortuary...I know you said the city contracts with the mortuary for indigent victims, but...isn't any business paid for with city funds public record?"

"Actually, yes," Kerri said, impressed by my knowledge.

"So that means, you could request an accounting

or an audit of how much was paid to the mortuary over the years," I said.

"You're onto something except, I couldn't exactly order an audit without getting my ass fired. However, a tax-paying citizen could ask without penalty."

"Great. We just need to find some respectable person to ask for an audit and then—"

"And then wait two years for it to happen," Dylan interjected with a frown. "Nothing moves fast in the city except for the traffic. Have you ever tried to pull a permit for downtown? It's a fucking nightmare. The red tape is stupid, and that's just for a food cart."

"How do you know this?" I asked, intrigued.

She waved away my question, muttering, "One of Badger's terrible ideas. He thought he could use a food cart as a front to move product, but the red tape was more of a hassle than it was worth. I told him from the start it was a dumbass idea, but Badger had something to prove, I guess. Or he just really enjoyed watching me waste my time on useless errands."

My money was on the latter. I couldn't see Badger giving two shits about being a food cart owner, but I could see him running Dylan all around the city for a project he had no plans to operate.

"Was he going to offer dirty water dogs or hot,

roasted peanuts?" I teased, breaking into a smart-ass grin.

"Dogs," Dylan answered, laughing at the memory. "So fucking stupid."

It felt good to laugh about something as average as every day, normal-people shit.

Most people worried about mundane details that in the big scheme of things didn't matter at all. We had to worry about how to stay alive, take down a human trafficking network, and think about a possible future when neither of us had much of a foundation to stand on.

When life was handing out lemons...yeah, I got a bushel, but hey, I guess I had to learn how to grab some tequila and salt to make the best of it, right?

Kerri smiled and shook her head at us, admitting, "We might not have the time a citizen-generated audit might take, but maybe Hicks can get us what we're looking for. I'll talk to him tonight about it."

"You're meeting up with Hicks?" I asked, interested.

"Before you get the wrong idea, it's about the case," Kerri assured me.

But Dylan and I both started snickering.

Kerri frowned, shaking her head. "Sometimes I forget you're both still kids. Trust me, there's nothing between Hicks and I. He was a good detective back in the day, and I respect his skills. There's nothing more."

"That's good because my Gran once told me, don't waste time trying to paint those red flags green because eventually, the red always comes bleeding through."

"Wise woman," Kerri murmured with a small smile as she repeated more firmly, "there's nothing between Hicks and I. Now, let's focus, please."

Kerri's refusal to admit she had feelings for Hicks was similar to Dylan's unhealthy connection to Badger.

Maybe it was a blessing that I probably wouldn't live long enough to suffer through a toxic relationship that ended up twisting my understanding of life and the expectation of love.

Or maybe — good, bad, or indifferent — it was just another rite of passage that I'd never get to experience.

13

The good news was that Hicks managed to finagle credentials, but the bad news was he only managed to get one. It made sense to me that I would be the one to take the risk, but Dylan thought that was a shit plan.

"There's no way she's going in by herself, and you're an asshole if you let her," she said.

I got that Dylan was protective, but I didn't need her picking a fight with Hicks over something stupid. "He's not the boss of me, and neither are you. Franklin was my buyer, so I'll be the one to take the risk. You know that if it was your buyer in question, there's nothing that would stop you from taking this job."

Dylan refused to see my point. "That's totally different. I can handle myself."

I narrowed my stare, bristling at her statement. "So can I."

"No offense, but Franklin nearly dragged you out a side door the other night. What happens if he shows up while you're playing a maid? Are you going to let him drag you into his bedroom, or are you going to fucking take him down?"

"I'll take care of it," I answered, hardening my voice. I didn't need Dylan to remind me how I fucked up. I was very aware, and it wouldn't happen again. I returned to Hicks, getting to business. "Tell me how this works."

Hicks nodded, moving on, not the least bit ruffled by Dylan's outburst. "All right, you're going in as a new hire with this temp agency that provides employees for the cleaning service Dubois uses. You'll be training with another person. So, you'll have to go by the temp agency and sign some paperwork. I've got a fake ID for you, but try not to answer too many questions. Don't volunteer anything that you don't have to."

I accepted the slick new license with a shake of my head, peeping at the totally fake persona created for me. "This isn't my first rodeo," I murmured, but wrinkled my nose at the details. I definitely didn't look like an 'Erin,' which was the name stamped on the ID. *Oh well. Beggars couldn't be choosers, so here we go.* "What are they expecting?"

"It's real simple. You're the new girl learning the ropes. When you're in there, that's when you keep your eyes peeled and look for anything that we talked about. Pictures, documentation, anything in the hard file. Don't worry about the computer because it's not likely he's dumb enough to keep anything incriminating on a digital file."

Dylan piped in, "What's she supposed to do if Franklin shows up? Just smile and say, 'Hey, what up, fucker?'"

Hicks regarded Dylan with irritation but answered, "According to my source, he shouldn't be there at all. He prefers to be away from the cleaning crew when they are there."

"Not surprising. I can't imagine that prick *deigning* to mingle with the help. It's beneath him," I said, but that worked for me. I wasn't ready to face him again after what happened at the fundraiser. I couldn't trust that I wouldn't launch myself at his face with a cleaver.

I was there to collect information, not his scalp — at least not yet.

"Fine, let's do this," I said, pocketing my ID. "When am I supposed to report to the temp agency?"

Hicks looked at his watch. "You need to be there in about an hour, so you should get ready to leave."

Dylan popped from the sofa with a determined set of her jaw. "Well, I'm going with you to the temp agency," she said, daring either of us to stop her. "For all, they know I could just be a friend looking for a job, too."

Hicks shrugged. "That's fine just keep yourself in check and don't blow her cover."

Dylan snorted, "This isn't my first rodeo either. I know how to blend."

"See that you do," Hicks said, adding gruffly, "And stay out of trouble."

"Thanks, *Dad*," Dylan quipped with a sour expression, but I sensed that Dylan wasn't entirely salty about Hicks' warning because sometimes it felt good to know that someone cared.

Security at the temp agency was laughable. They barely looked at my documentation, gave my application a stamp of approval, and sent me off to the cleaning service office for my badge, uniform, and assignment.

Dylan and I parted ways as soon as we reached

the cleaning business, and I connected with my cleaning partner, a girl who was only a few years old than me, named Macy.

"It's nice to have a partner again," Macy gushed as we jumped on the elevator for Franklin's Tribeca loft. My nerves were strung tight, but I put on a good front, smiling as if I were happy to be there. "We lost the last girl because she got a better job someplace else, though I can't say I blame her. Maxi Maids isn't exactly throwing hundred dollar bills our way despite the ritzy clientele we serve."

"Does Maxi Maids have a high turn-over?" I asked, watching the floor buttons light up as we climbed higher. Of course, Franklin would live at the top. Penthouse living was definitely his style.

"Well, kinda. Maxi Maids is kinda known for hiring people without, um, documentation if you know what I mean. So, they never stay for too long, but I really thought the last girl was going to stick around. I guess you never know when a better opportunity is just around the corner."

Macy's chirping was irritating, but she seemed harmless and not likely to pay too close attention to what I was doing, which would work in my favor.

"You are in for a treat," Macy said, sliding the keycard that opened the entrance to an open floor plan, expansive and luxuriant living space. "Can you believe that some people live like this? My tiny studio is smaller than the guest bathroom. C'mon, I'll give you a quick tour."

I pretended to be impressed for Macy's sake and to keep her from suspecting I wasn't there to scrub his toilets, but I noted every detail as I followed her around.

Pristine white sofa set with off-white throw pillows, pale hardwood floors and standing art sculptures that made good conversational pieces during his fancy dinner parties — if only the evidence of his crimes were as easily put on display as his obscene wealth.

That would've made my mission a lot easier.

"Mr. Dubois has the nicest loft of all our clients. I love cleaning this place," she shared as I trailed behind her. She continued with a conspiratorial whisper, "Sometimes I like to pretend that Mr. Dubois happens upon me while I'm cleaning and we fall madly in love. You know, kind of like a *Pretty Woman* thing except I'm not a prostitute. Or maybe *Maid in Manhattan* would be more fitting. I know it's stupid, but it helps pass the time when I'm cleaning."

I fake smiled as if I agreed. The idea of being

anywhere near Franklin Dubois made me want to vomit. But then she didn't know him like I did. She didn't know that he was a sadistic bastard. And she definitely didn't see that he was more than likely a killer.

"So how long have you been cleaning Mr. Dubois's place?" I asked, feigning interest. "He must really trust you."

She laughed. "Oh, he doesn't know me at all, but he does trust the agency. We've had his account for at least three years. Before that, I don't know who had his account, but I've been working for the agency for five years, and I remember when he became a client. Anyway, I've always enjoyed cleaning here. It's always spotless anyway, so it's not even like we have to do a deep clean. Some rich people are disgusting. I'm talking like they're freaking animals. They're so used to people cleaning up after them that they've forgotten basic human decency."

I wanted to murmur, "you have no idea," but I kept that to myself.

It didn't surprise me that Franklin kept an immaculate home. The man had very particular ideas about how things should be done and how they should be handled. I have no doubt those ideas also extended to his living quarters.

"So speaking of a Mrs. Dubois, is he married?"

Macy giggled. "Oh, are you interested in the job?"

Fuck no. I swallowed my revulsion. "No, I was just curious. Guys like him usually have someone attached to them, right?"

"Well, I don't know if he's married, but I do know that he has kids."

That was the information I was interested in. "Oh? How do you know?"

Macy motioned for me to follow. We went into a room that looked like a home office. Multiple framed photos of two young girls smiling for the camera graced the white birch credenza behind the desk. Beautiful, perfectly lovely girls who had probably never experienced a fraction of their father's wickedness.

At least, for their sake, I hoped not.

I appeared at the pictures. "So pretty," I murmured. "He must be so proud."

She sighed. "He has what seems like a perfect life. So it stands to reason he probably has a perfect wife, too. One can dream, right?"

I wanted to tell her that anything involving Franklin would be a nightmare, but why ruin her fantasy with reality?

"Well, I'm going to start on the kitchen if you want to tidy up in here that's fine with me."

That actually worked out perfectly because this was where I wanted to be.

Everything about the loft spoke of luxury and wealth. I didn't know the names or brands of anything around me, but I knew the contents of this room probably cost more than I would ever see in a lifetime.

Franklin had bragged about his European connections like he was some kind of royalty, but I had no idea what he did for a living. He hadn't told me his real name, and it wasn't like he'd been trying to make a real connection with me. *Thank God.*

The things he did to me were locked away in the deepest, darkest corner of my mind. There were some nights I still woke up in a cold sweat, shaking all over, my arms wrapped around myself in a tight ball.

I hadn't been under some misguided notion that my first time was going to be something out of a fairy-tale, but I hadn't expected to be horrifically violated in so many different ways.

The physical aspect of the abuse I could probably get over eventually. It was the way he'd gotten into my head that was the ultimate cruelty.

He'd played the part of the gentle billionaire who cared. I didn't buy into his act, but I knew there were probably girls who had.

When he realized I wasn't going to play his game, that's when things got really bad. Maybe that's why he'd made the offer to elevate. I shuddered to think of the cruelty he'd had in mind for act two.

I pretended to dust, but I was looking for anything that might be useful. I could hear Macy's voice throughout the loft, calling out instructions, but I ignored her. I wasn't there to make his loft spic and span. I was there to find something that would destroy him.

Rows of books filled the library, which made me wonder if he was an attorney of some sort. The pale, bleached maple desk gleamed even before I started polishing, but the lemon scent triggered a memory that nearly sent me to my knees.

His playroom. That massive four-poster bed. The armoire filled with whips, chains, even knives. An overwhelming array of sexual toys and torture devices at his fingertips. Everything polished to a high shine and smelling faintly of lemon.

I swallowed the bile trapped in my throat. *Get it together, Nicole.* I couldn't fall apart every single time I was faced with the past. If I was going to squash this motherfucker, I had to toughen up. No more freezing. No more crying. No more weakness. I had to be more like Dylan. Hard. Jaded. Willing to slit a motherfucker's throat if push came to shove.

I refocused with purpose. There had to be something in this loft worth taking. Something that gave away his guilt. My gaze snagged on the framed photo of his daughters. One of them looked the same age as me. We shared similar bone structure. To an untrained eye, we could've been sisters.

Maybe that was the reason why he'd been so interested in me, willing to pay whatever price Madame Marie had demanded. I looked like his daughter. Or close enough that he could close his eyes and imagine that he was doing those horrible things to her without actually paying the price of incest by violating his own flesh and blood.

I picked up the frame and stared. It was impossible to tell by the photo what kind of life they lived away from the public eye, but something told me he was a doting father to these two precious princesses.

He had no reservations against being a horrible monster to someone he had no ties to. Somehow seeing this picture made things that much worse. I replaced the photo with deliberate care, fighting the urge to smash it to pieces.

I agreed with Hicks. Franklin was the type who would want momentoes. Something that he could revisit when he didn't have someone locked in his playroom. He would need someplace safe and hidden for his treasures.

I slowly turned. Around the room looking for anything that seemed out of place or struck a chord. My gaze returned to the large fractal painting behind the desk, above the credenza. The deep golds, reds, and oranges blended in a passionate dance that seemed sexual to me even though there was nothing overtly suggestive.

It was also shockingly bold in a room that was otherwise a palette of different shades of white.

I cocked my head, musing. Was he that cliche as to hide his safe behind that painting? Hiding in plain view? I stepped forward and carefully lifted the artwork from the wall.

Zero points for originality.

I'd found his treasure chest.

Now, all I had to do was find a way to open it.

14

Macy startled me when she popped into the room. I froze, thinking she was going to rat me out, but instead, she looked excited that I'd found something she already knew about.

"Ha! You found his secret safe! I found it in the first week. I know it's wrong, but I'm super nosy. I was dusting, and I thought the painting looked a little off, and then when I went to straighten it, I realized there was something behind it. Pretty exciting stuff. Someday I want to be rich enough to have a secret room. Feels so mysterious. Although my secret room would probably just have craft stuff in it."

Lora would react this way — utterly oblivious to the danger or the import of what she'd found. I forced a smile, agreeing with her. "Yeah, that's exactly how I found it, too. Now I kinda wish I could take a peek inside. I mean, what could he be hiding in there?"

Macy waved away my question. "Oh, I'm sure it's just extra cash and bonds and shit like that. I mean, that's what the rich people in the movies always hide. Never know when you need a little extra, right?"

I would bet my life there was more than cash in that safe, but I played along. "For real," I agreed but added, "I guess I'm just terminally nosy because I have to know what's inside. I mean, I would never steal from the guy, but doesn't it kill you not to know what he's got in there?"

"A little," Macy agreed with a tiny giggle as if this were all a game. "But I'm sure he has a super-secret password. There's no way to get into that thing without tripping the alarm."

I returned my attention to the safe. Sure enough, it was wired with an alarm system. *Damn it.* I nodded, pretending to let it go. Macy smiled and said, "I'm going to tackle the kitchen. Mr. Dubois likes his countertops to shine like they're brand new. It's the only job that takes a few minutes more than the rest of the house. Since you're new, I'll do it this time around, but next time, it's all you, girl."

I nodded, accepting that deal, relieved when she bounced out of the room like the human version of Tigger the Tiger.

Once she was clear, I narrowed my gaze at that safe. I couldn't leave without opening that thing. I knew in my bones, there was something worth finding in that wall box.

People were notoriously clumsy with personal information. I turned and opened the drawers, looking for anything that might give away a hiding spot for his password. My gaze snagged again on the framed photos of his kids. Aside from the picture with the two girls, there was a photo of his oldest, by herself, at a birthday party. I moved closer. There was an inscription on the frame. It read: *The day you were born, I was blessed.*"

And then there was a date: 05-08-08

That icky feeling returned, and I had to take the chance that my gut was right.

I wiped my sweaty palms on my thighs before reaching for the dial. I said a prayer to a God I wasn't sure I believed in and then slowly turned the dial to the numbers on the inscription. I was taking a considerable risk. If I tripped the alarm, I had to be ready to run like my ass was on fire. My heart slammed against my breastbone and thumped in my eardrum.

I squeezed my eyes shut as I made the final turn. A tiny *snick* told me my gamble had paid off.

I swallowed my squeal of victory and opened the safe door. My hands shook as I pulled out the paper contents. Two stacks of cash, a bunch of financial documents, and a plain ledger marked with one word that stopped my heart.

Avalon.

I started to shake, but I didn't have time to celebrate. I stuffed the ledger into my shirt and reached for a manilla envelope, shaking the contents out quickly.

I nearly dropped the envelope in horror when I saw what came tumbling out.

Pictures.

Lots of them.

My vision blurred. I picked up the ones that'd fallen to the floor and stuffed them back inside the envelope, terrified of what I might see.

I didn't remember Franklin taking pictures of me.

But I was in that stack.

I wanted to throw up.

I wanted to burn them all.

I wanted to collapse to the floor and cry for my stolen innocence, dignity, and humanity.

Instead, I carefully stuffed everything back into the envelope. I then shoved the envelope into the back of my pants, hidden by my smock.

I slowly and quietly returned everything else before closing the safe door and replacing the painting.

My heart was still hammering when Macy burst into the room looking panicked as she said, "Oh my God, he's here! He never shows up when Maxi Maids is booked for his service." At first, I mistook her panic for one of fear until she started scrambling for a mirror to check her hair. I wanted to slap the stupidity out of her, but I didn't have time to mess with her. I had to get out of there before Franklin saw me.

"I don't feel good. Maybe I should leave before I throw up all over your hard work," I said, trying to hide my desperation, but sweat had started to bead my brow.

"Eww. You don't look so good," Macy agreed. "If Latasha finds out you came to work sick, she'll have a shit fit. I don't want you to get fired on your first day. I like you," she said winking.

I nodded, feeling the moments tick by with

heavy finality. "Can you distract him or something while I slip out?"

"Yeah, I think so. I mean, we're not supposed to talk to the client, but I can probably bend the rules a little bit."

"Yes, thank you. I really need this job." I bobbed my head, so grateful. I watched as she motioned for me to follow, gesturing for me to wait, and then when the coast was clear, told me to book it out the front door.

I didn't wait. I ran for the door, listening with fear as Franklin's voice carried through the loft. He sounded angry. "Where's the fucking girl who was in my office?" he said to Macy, and my blood froze. He must've had a camera installed, and he'd seen me get into his safe.

"She wasn't feeling too good, Mr. Dubois so I sent her home—"

"Goddamn it!" he roared. "I want her brought back right now!"

He knew it was me. I was terrified for stupid, hapless Macy, who had no idea she was closed in with a monster, but I couldn't do anything to save her. I had to hope that she had some sense and got out of there before he did something awful and had The Avalon take care of the body.

The elevator doors closed just as Franklin reentered the living room, his face contorted with rage. I didn't think he saw me, but I wasn't taking the chance. Sweat poured from my body as I burst from the elevator on the ground floor and ran like the devil was on my heels because he was.

I clutched the precious packages to my body as I ran, nearly skidding down the stairs of the subway to jump onto the next train. I had to get as far away from Franklin as possible.

I couldn't stop looking in every direction, so terrified I was going to see Franklin on my tail, but I managed to make it back to Hicks' apartment without being grabbed. I slammed the door behind me and fumbled with the slide lock and deadbolt, my hands were shaking so bad.

It wasn't until I had successfully locked the door that I let myself slide to the floor in a heap, breathing hard and nearly bawling. Dylan flew to my side, scared and worried as she barked, "Did he fucking touch you?"

I shook my head and handed Hicks the packages as I gulped back sobs. I gestured wildly. "I found something. I found something!"

Hicks didn't wait and ripped open the envelope. Photos spilled onto his desk. His eyes widened when he realized what he was looking at. I knew the minute he saw mine.

His gaze lifted, and Dylan rose to join him. When she saw the pictures, she swore with murderous intent. "That sick motherfucker. He took photos of the girls he bought and abused." Dylan paused to lift one picture in particular. She cocked her head, processing what she saw.

"Is it…Nova?" I asked fearfully.

Dylan shook her head, showing me the picture.

My gaze widened, surprised. I slowly climbed to my feet and peered at the photo. She was younger, afraid, and less polished, but there was no mistaking the bone structure of that haughty bitch.

The one who threatened to starve me until I agreed to elevate.

Fucking Olivia.

"I knew she was an auction girl, but I had no idea she was one of Franklin's," I said, trying to make sense of what I knew. "Why would she force me to elevate when she knew how awful Franklin was?"

"That's how Madame Moirai operates…either you elevate, or you end up in the ground. Obviously, at some point, Olivia must've played the part of the dutiful slave girl, and she was returned to Madame

Moirai at some point when Franklin tired of playing with her."

"Talk about Stockholm Syndrome," I murmured in disgust. "I know I should feel sorry for her...but I can't."

Although seeing that picture of her, as broken and bruised as I'd been in the same situation, created some conflicting feelings that I didn't want to acknowledge.

"Fuck her, she was willing to feed you to the wolf to save her own skin," Dylan said, moving back to the stack to take a better look. I knew she was searching for Nova, and I held my breath, afraid that she would find her, afraid that she wouldn't.

"See anyone else you recognize?" Hicks asked in his signature gravelly voice.

Dylan shook her head. "No."

I breathed a secret sigh of relief. I knew it would've made our job a little easier if Nova had been in that stack, but I didn't think Dylan could take that news right now.

Hicks had moved onto the ledger. "Holy shit," he murmured in the first real expression of shock I'd ever seen on his craggy face. "How'd you get this?"

I gulped. "It was in his office. I figured out the code for his secret safe and took it, but he knows it was me. I guess he had a camera in his office. He got there just as I managed to make it out. It's only a matter of time before he tracks me back here. I didn't have time to disguise myself from the CCTV."

"What is it?" Dylan asked.

"It looks like a financial record of every dime ever spent at one of those auctions. And it's a fuck-ton."

My shoulders sagged with relief. Maybe this nightmare was finally over.

"This right here is dynamite. We gotta get this someplace safe," he said, eyeing the ledger like it was poisonous. "He'll do anything to keep this from landing in the hands of someone who can fuck up his life."

"Like us," Dylan said, grinning. "Let's take it to the cops."

"No, we can't trust this with the local cops. The Avalon has the cops in their pocket. No, I need to talk to Kerri before we do anything with this, but first, we need to get you someplace safe. He's going to come for you."

I shook at the memory of Franklin's expression when he realized I'd gotten out of his loft with his incriminating shit. "But this is going to save us, right? I mean, we were looking for hard evidence, and here it is. This is what we needed," I said, desperately needing to hear that this was almost over.

Hicks wouldn't answer. Instead, he stuffed the ledger and the pictures into his backpack and told us to pack because we were leaving right now.

My stomach clenched with fear.

This wasn't over for us.

I think it might've just gotten worse.

15

Kerri decided the city was too hot for us now that Franklin knew I'd stolen his property and made the decision to relocate from Hicks' place to someplace upstate.

"I own my parents' place out near Esterdell. We can crash there for the time being. It's been closed up for the winter, so the pipes might be frozen, but it's the best I can do on such short notice. I can't risk booking a hotel room when they might track my credit card straight to you. No one knows about my parent's place. We should be safe."

"I have a job with Badger. I can't go hole up in the sticks," Dylan said, shaking her head. "Besides, I'm not going nowhere without WiFi."

Kerri shot Dylan a dark look at the mention of

Badger. She'd asked us to stop running jobs, which hadn't been a significant tragedy on my end, but Dylan never listened to anyone, not even her own little voice of reason. I wasn't surprised when Dylan kept slipping out in the middle of the night, but there was nothing I could do to stop her.

"I would've thought that after almost getting you killed, you would've found a reason to steer clear of Badger," Kerri said.

Dylan shrugged. "It's just business."

"Yeah, well, that business got a man killed. It was plain fucking dumb luck that the gun wasn't recovered at the scene, and no one seems particularly keen to chase after the killer of a drug dealer."

I didn't feel bad for the man I killed. I was disconnected from the actions of that night. Probably going to need a shit ton of therapy at some point, but who had time to think of that now? Certainly not me.

"Lady Luck is finally on my side," I murmured, sharing a small smile with Dylan even though I should've sided with Kerri.

"Lady Luck has a tendency to set people up with a false sense of security, which ends up getting young girls caught up in shit they can't control."

"I can take care of myself," Dylan retorted, digging her heels in. Dylan had issues with authority. She always would. Kerri trying to control Dylan's actions was an exercise in futility.

Hicks stepped in with firm authority, saying to Dylan, "Stop being a shit. You're going."

"Yeah, and who's going to make me?" Dylan challenged.

"If I have to, me. If you want to be self-destructive after we've taken care of this Avalon business, that's on you. Until then, I'm going to keep you safe, whether you like it or not. Now, get your fucking stuff."

I expected a blowout, but the building bristle in Dylan's energy suddenly dissipated like a storm cloud unable to withstand the wind pushing it from the sky. Dylan scowled but spun on her heel to disappear into the bedroom.

I released a pent-up breath, exchanging a look with Kerri. I had no doubt that Hicks would've thrown Dylan over his shoulder and dragged her screaming ass to the vehicle, but it would've been a spectacle we didn't need.

We were packed and ready to go within minutes. We piled into Kerri's vehicle and hit the road without looking back. I'd never call myself partial to the country having grown up in the city, but there was a calm away from the chaos that allowed me to breathe.

Dylan, on the other hand, couldn't stand the quiet.

"We won't have to worry about The Avalon taking us out because I'm literally going to die of boredom," she complained as we climbed from the car after an hour and a half drive. Fresh snow blanketed the area. The air smelled crisp and fresh. I drew a deep breath and took solace in the fact that no hidden cameras were hiding in the trees, waiting to capture our picture and blast that information to Madame Moirai and her henchmen.

Maybe when this was all over, I'd find myself a quiet town in the mountains and happily spend my life doing country stuff. Whatever that might be. Gardening? Raising chickens? Who knows? All I knew was that it wouldn't include running from people trying to kill me.

"You grew up here?" I asked, taking in the quiet and relative isolation. I tried to picture a young Kerri and her sister running around this place, playing in mud puddles and making snow angels. "It's nice."

"Yeah, it was," Kerri said, but she didn't look any happier to be holing up in her childhood home than Dylan was to be cooped up among the trees. There were probably a lot of ghosts lurking in every corner for Kerri. I felt terrible for putting her in this position, but there wasn't much I could do but try to ride it out.

That's what we were all doing.

Kerri opened up the house and stamped the snow from shoes in the mudroom before going in.

The house smelled of old wood, dust, and time. The hardwood floors creaked beneath our feet as Kerri gave us the short tour. The house wasn't small, but it wasn't overly big either. It felt homey even though it was evident by the layer of dust covering everything, no one had stepped foot in this house in a long time.

"So, I guess you don't come here very often?" I surmised, lighting dragging my finger through the thick coating on every surface. "I mean, it's probably hard with your sister and everything, right?"

"Yeah, a lot of memories between these walls."

Hicks cleared his throat and said, "I'll go bring in the bags" before bailing. Hicks wasn't exactly the deepest of men. Anything that smacked of emotional depth sent him running.

It was probably why he was an alcoholic. A lot to unpack in that brain and no tools to deal with whatever was squatting in his memories.

I looked forward to the day when I didn't have to pay witnesses to other people's emotional baggage.

If I survived this, I think I'd become a hermit. I didn't want to care about anyone but myself.

I'd never considered myself a selfish person, but I was starting to understand why it was better to simply worry about *Numero Uno.*

But that would have to wait.

Hicks volunteered to grab some food at the local grocery store while we helped Kerri open up the house and put the bedding together. Dylan and I opted to share a bedroom while Kerri and Hicks would take the other two available rooms.

I wasn't going to say anything about the bedroom situation, but Dylan couldn't help herself. "How come you and Hicks ain't gonna shack up together? You know you want to."

Kerri cast an annoyed glance Dylan's way as she finished smoothing the comforter over the bed. "Cut it out, smart-ass. I've already told you, it's not like that between Hicks and me. We're friends. That's it."

"So, what's wrong with friends-with-benefits?" Dylan asked. "You're not getting any younger. I would've thought you'd jump at any chance to get that D."

I ignored Dylan, irritated for Kerri's sake, but

also because Dylan's careless comment rubbed at a raw nerve.

"Just drop it, Dylan," I growled, feeling the walls starting to crowd me in the small room.

"I'm just saying—"

I glared, heat prickling around my ears. "Shut the fuck up already."

I tuned out as Dylan and Kerri started to bicker about stupid shit.

I hated the idea of sex with anyone. I hadn't realized what I was giving up when I sold myself for what I thought was going to be a night that I could forget.

But I understood now.

The thought of anyone touching me ever again... it made me physically ill.

Would I ever be normal again? Sex was a natural expectation of a relationship. How could I explain to a potential partner that the idea of letting someone else touch me sexually made me want to run and hide in a corner?

I swallowed the lump in my throat, hating the memory of Franklin's hands on me. Hating that for a split second, my body had betrayed me with tiny spikes of pleasure before it all went to hell. I didn't have anyone I could talk to about that part of what'd happened to me.

Not that I would.

"I need some air," I said abruptly, leaving Dylan and Kerri behind to bolt from the house. My head was a mess. One little stupid comment from Dylan, and I'm triggered like a mental case.

I shook out my trembling hands and blew on them as the cold winter air nibbled at my exposed skin.

Would there ever come a time when winter weather didn't remind me of the night we fled the auction house? I wanted to hook my brain up to a giant computer and do a complete cleanse of everything that'd happened to me from top to bottom.

I didn't want to remember anything.

Not even Lora.

To be honest, my memories of Lora felt like they belonged to someone else. I didn't recognize that person anymore.

I sank down onto the wooden steps and hugged my knees to my chest. Birds chirped in the trees, oblivious to anything below them. Tiny, unseen critters or bugs rustled in the fallen, sodden leaves not covered by snowfall. An old wood shack sheltered a stack of wood that looked aged and weathered but remained dry and untouched by the recent storm.

My breath plumed in front of me, and my ass was already starting to lose sensation from the chill.

To my surprise, Dylan came outside and sat beside me. For a long moment, she said nothing. She knew what had triggered me without me having to tell her.

Maybe it was that mutual trauma thing at work.

She leaned over, nudging me with her shoulder. "Sorry," she said, her tone contrite. "I shouldn't have said that."

I shrugged, playing it off even though tears were filling my eyes. "It's nothing."

"It's something, and we've both got it. I don't know why I said that to Kerri. Sometimes I can't help the shit that just pops out."

"I know."

"Makes me mad," Dylan admitted in an agonized whisper. "I was never scared of sex before. I just thought, whatever, it's just sex. I never realized it would be so...horrible."

"Me, either." I wiped my eyes and voiced the fear in my heart. "What if it never gets better? What if we *always* hate sex because of what happened to us?"

Dylan lifted her shoulders in a forlorn gesture, unsure. "I try not to think about it."

How could I forget, Dylan only focused on the here and now. I tried to do that, too, but for some reason, my brain wanted to push things a little further. As unlikely as it was, I tried to imagine a future.

And that future included meeting someone, right?

"We were raped," I said, saying the word out loud, starting to shake all over. "What they did to us...I don't know how to get past it. What if I never can? I don't want to be broken for the rest of my life."

Dylan wrapped her arms around me, hugging me tightly. "We'll find a way."

I sniffed back tears. "And what if we don't?"

"Then we become those crazy old spinsters who have too many cats, and their apartment always smells like piss and Meow Mix."

I chuckled. "Are you saying we're going to live together as old ladies? That's a scary thought. Maybe we should just try therapy first."

"Fuck that. I'll take the cats."

I laughed, leaning against Dylan. "We're a fucked up bunch, aren't we?"

"Hell yeah, but maybe that's what makes us special."

"I don't feel special."

"Shut your face. You're special to me." I lifted my head to peer at Dylan. She wiped at her eyes and warned, "If you make me repeat it, I'll fucking punch you in the lady dick."

"A declaration of affection and the promise of violence all in one breath...God, Dylan, my life would be so dull without you."

"Damn straight, and don't you forget it."

I never could.

I never would.

Dylan and I were bound for life. We would kill for each other.

I bet Madame Moirai never counted on that little wrinkle.

Fuck her.

She'd created the monsters — and they were hungry for her blood.

16

After a good night's sleep, we tackled the envelope of pictures. At the same time, Hicks took the ledger and tried to figure out real identities tied to the purchases.

Kerri made fresh coffee and opened a package of pastries to share. Dylan poured enough sugar and cream in her coffee to turn into a dessert and then gobbled two pastries without missing a beat. My stomach couldn't handle the liquid octane with a sugar boost this early in the morning.

Not to mention, the task ahead of us stomped any hint of appetite from my gut.

As Hicks took more time to study the entries, it seemed Franklin operated as some kind of private accountant for the secret network.

Only, there weren't real names, only nicknames, so without the corresponding legend to match purchases to identities, it was another puzzle we had to try and put together. The buyers were either "Mr." Or "Madame" along with a corresponding nickname. For example, together we figured out that Franklin Dubois' name was Mr. White, because of his evident penchant for overwhelmingly white furniture in his loft.

The sheer number of entries in that ledger made me want to throw it against the wall. Every nickname represented a human being willing to do depraved things to a kid.

Every sum of money represented a kid purchased.

I shouldn't have been surprised that there were women on that ledger seeing as Madame Moirai was the queen bee of the network, but somehow it felt worse knowing that women were betraying their own gender.

"I'm going to make some calls," Hicks said, scooping up the ledger and his cup of black coffee. He looked rough this morning, likely because there wasn't any booze in the house, and he usually doctored his morning cup of Joe with some whiskey. Even though it was better for him to skip the liquor, I felt bad for him because going cold turkey must suck balls.

I gave him props for being willing to suffer through the cravings to keep Kerri happy. I knew enough about addicts to understand that no one quit their drug of choice for someone else, but I recognized that he was trying, even if it was doomed to be a short window of sobriety.

I'm sure Kerri knew, too, but she didn't say anything. I supposed we all took what we could get in certain situations.

As I watched Hicks walk stiffly from the room, I knew he didn't want to sift through the photos with us. Maybe it was because he had a daughter, or perhaps it was too disturbing to see my photos in that stack, but either way, he had no stomach for that job and left it to us.

Not that I was jumping for joy at the prospect of staring at that horrid bundle of pain and torture either, but I was getting better at compartmentalizing disturbing shit.

"Is it me, or do some of these girls seem really young?" I asked, peering at one of the photos trying to put some distance between the image and the reality of what it was. For all I knew, the girl in this photo was dead.

Kerri took a look, agreeing with me, her expression pensive. "I was just thinking the same thing."

"If these girls aren't eighteen, doesn't that make, like what they did, a bigger crime?" Dylan asked. "Isn't there some kind of major penalty if they're selling kids?"

"Absolutely, but until we can get IDs on these girls, I have no idea who they are or if they are juveniles," Kerri said, frowning. "You said you recognized one of the girls?"

I nodded. "Yes, her name is Olivia. Or at least that's what we know her by."

"Yeah, fucking little bitch. She practically starved Jilly and me."

I nodded, remembering. "She threatened to starve me, too, if I didn't agree to Franklin's offer to elevate. And come to find out she was Franklin's auction girl, too? That woman's got some brass balls."

Kerri tried to play devil's advocate. "People who have been trafficked often get stuck in the lifestyle, either by force or by choice, but sometimes that choice is an illusion. They get brainwashed into thinking that the life they live is the only one available to them. You have to remember that as much as you might hate this girl, she was a victim, too."

I didn't care. I couldn't forgive her. I replied,

without emotion. "If I see that bitch again, I'll kill her."

And I meant it.

"Get in line," Dylan quipped with a dark look. "I fucking hate oatmeal on a good day, much less being force-fed that slop just to survive."

"It wasn't just the food or the cruelty. It was the way she looked at me...like I was nothing but a commodity. She was a cold-ass cunt, and I don't care what she's been through, it doesn't give her a pass for what she did."

I had no forgiveness in my heart for Olivia. She was in a position of power. At any given point, she could've saved countless other girls from meeting the same fate. She had just as much blood on her hands as Madame Moirai, if not more. Nothing anyone could say would ever change my mind on that score.

Kerri was too smart to try and convince me to feel differently, so she moved on. "I can't exactly run these photos through the database at my own station. Too many eyes are on me. However, I might be able to pull some strings with the local police department to use their computers. We might be able to get a hit on the missing persons database."

"What happens if we find that these missing girls

are on the database?" I asked. "When can we go to the cops with what we know?"

I was chomping at the bit. We finally had something solid to pin Madame Moirai and her fucking perverts to the wall, and we were sitting on it. None of that made sense to me. In my opinion, we should've been gift-wrapping all we had and delivering it to the authorities — like as in, yesterday.

Kerri explained with a patient tone. "We have to build a solid case. As big as this information is, it's still not enough to take down a network as vast as The Avalon. We need big guns. Possibly even the FBI. I don't know how far Madame Moirai's reach is and until I can find someone I trust, this information stays with us."

"Yeah, but we've all got prices on our heads at this point. The longer we hold onto this time bomb, the bigger chance it's going to blow up in our face," I argued.

Dylan agreed. "I say we bundle up all this shit and take it to the bigwigs like you said. Someone in the FBI has to be high enough up the chain to handle this kind of thing. I mean, how are we supposed to shoulder the burden of a bust like this? They go to school to learn how to deal with this shit, not us."

Kerri sighed. "I hear what you're saying, just give

me a chance to do what I can first. I understand this is scary, and it seems like an open-and-shut case now that we have these photos and the ledger, but I'm telling you, I've seen cases with better evidence get thrown out on a technicality. I don't want that to happen. If that happens, we're all as good as dead. We have one shot, and we can't blow it because we're impatient."

"Easy for you to say. No one's creeping into your bedroom at night to slit your throat," Dylan shot back, getting up and walking away. I didn't want to rip into Kerri, but Dylan was right. She had no idea what we'd lost in this fight. Jilly sacrificed herself to save us. That kind of weight wasn't something you got to put down because it was heavy. As long as I lived, I would never be free of Jilly's sacrifice — and neither would Dylan.

"We need this to be over," I said. "We're tired of running and tired of being afraid."

Kerri reached across the table to place her hand over mine, sympathetic and warm. "I know. I want this to be over too, but we have to do this right. Trust that I know what I'm doing. Please."

I wasn't used to people being on my side. I definitely wasn't used to someone looking out for my best interest. I felt awkward in the face of that genuine concern. I pulled my hand away. "Fine, but don't take too long," I muttered before rising and walking away.

I didn't want to be a jerk, but I agreed with Dylan. I didn't want to hold onto the evidence. I wanted to hand off the responsibility to someone who could handle the burden, so we didn't have to.

I didn't want to wear wigs or hide in the shadows anymore. I didn't want to run jobs for Badger like a street thug. I wanted to be a typical teenager with stupid teenage problems.

Whatever those were.

I wanted to sleep at night without jerking awake at the slightest sound, my heart hammering in my chest like a wild thing, as terror drenched my skin. I wanted it all to be over.

Is that so much to ask?

But if I took the time to step outside of my whiny pity-party, I knew Kerri was right. If we truly wanted this to be over, without anyone left to pick up where Madame Moirai left off, we had to be smart.

We had to obliterate this network so no one could ever pick up the pieces again. We had to expose every single disgusting piece of shit whoever crossed Madame Moirai's palms with cash so they could work out their perverted kinks and fantasies.

We had to be vigilant and strong when we wanted to be weak and reckless.

Our work wasn't finished, and we wouldn't be safe until we did precisely what Kerri was saying. I trusted her as much as I trusted anyone, but that didn't stop me from wanting to close my eyes and make it all go away.

I guess I was human.

But the fact of the matter was, I didn't claw my way out of the auction house and run away from everything I'd ever known just to give up now.

If I had to, I'd use my hatred to warm me when my heart felt cold and empty. I would use any tool necessary to achieve my goal.

In my mind's eye, I kept seeing Franklin's face, twisted with rage, as I escaped from his loft, and it no longer scared me. I would've given anything to have a gun in my hand at that moment. I would've blown his brains all over his expensive white furniture, splattering every surface with blood and gore.

I had no doubt at some point, Franklin would've killed me if I'd taken the offer to elevate.

Because I wasn't the kind of girl to say and do pleasing things like Olivia had to survive. My mouth had always gotten me into trouble. He would've tired of the novelty at some point, and he would've lost his temper, gone too far.

I'd already tasted the brutality of his frenzy, and it was a taste that would always leave bitterness in my mouth.

Even smart-assed, stubborn, hard-headed kids break at some point.

How quickly would I have broken? Would I have begged to die? Begged to live? Would I have prayed for help that would never come?

I hugged myself tightly against the wind chill cutting through my sweatshirt. I didn't need confirmation from a database to know that some of those girls hadn't been eighteen.

And the fear in their eyes had made them look that much younger than they probably were.

No one deserved to die like that.

I didn't know how this ended. I only knew that it would — one way or another.

If there was any chance Lady Luck was still smiling down on us, I hoped she had a little more luck in the tank reserved for the grand finale of our fucked up show.

Because I really wanted to win.

Even if the odds were against us.

I really wanted to live.

17

Hicks left later that day, saying he needed to head back to the city to talk with a forensic accountant he knew. While his reason was probably true, none of us were under the assumption that he wasn't dying for a drink.

Drunks always found a way to get their fix. Kerri knew the truth of it too, watching him leave with a sad, resigned expression.

"You know it's probably going to kill him someday," I said.

"I know."

She didn't waste energy, denying the truth. Kerri knew as well as anyone that running from the facts didn't make them less reliable. Whatever her feelings were for him, she didn't let them get in the way of doing what needed to be done.

Kerri squared her shoulders and shook off whatever she was feeling about Hicks and asked me, "Do you want to come with me?"

"To the police station?"

"Yeah, we'll just say you're job shadowing me, and my own station is currently under construction with a strict no outside visitors for the time being. It's a small station, no one will fact-check me."

"Seems like a security risk, but I like it," I said, intrigued.

I knew why she didn't ask Dylan. Dylan had zero interest in the legal side of things, but I was interested in taking a peek behind the curtain.

Not that I was destined to become a cop or anything, but something was satisfying about seeing real police work in action.

"Sure," I agreed, shrugging as if it were no big deal, but I liked that she'd asked me. "Can we pick up something to eat along the way?"

Kerri agreed with a smile. Dylan waved us off with disinterest, mumbling how she was going to take a nap. I felt weird leaving Dylan alone, but if anyone could take care of herself, it was that girl.

As we drove, I asked, "Is it crazy for you to be back in this town? I don't know what it's like to have my identity tied to a place. My mom and I moved around too much to get attached to anything. Not that I would've wanted to. All the places we lived in were shit holes. One apartment didn't even have running water. We had to brush our teeth with bottled water that we filled up in the bathroom of a gas station. It was pretty disgusting. I'm pretty sure I'm immune to every germ and virus known to man after drinking what tasted like toilet water."

Kerri grimaced. "I'm sorry. That's pretty shitty."

I barked a short laugh at her corny joke. "Yeah, it was."

She exhaled a long breath, answering, "It does feel weird to be here. Everything looks familiar and yet totally foreign at the same time. I was a different person when I lived here. My parents and I had a strained relationship, so my memories aren't exactly warm and fuzzy."

"Why? Were they dicks or something?"

"No, they weren't bad people. They were never cruel or abusive, but something within them died with my sister. I've seen it happen in other parents with a lost child. The loss changes them. It's not their fault, but it happens."

"Does that make you mad that they loved your sister more?"

"It's not that they loved her more. It's that the kids left behind have to deal with the fall-out of their parents' grief. It took me a long time to figure that out but once I did, all the anger just kinda went away. I guess that's when I stopped being self-destructive, but by then, our relationship wasn't the same anymore."

I thought of all the kids The Avalon had cut down and how they probably didn't have parents to miss them. Somehow that made their crime so much worse. Society had already shit on these kids, and then The Avalon came along and stomped them into the ground.

"What happens if we can find a kid in that database that wasn't an adult when they disappeared?" I asked.

"Crimes against children are in a different category. They get more attention."

"Let's say our hunch is right, and some of those girls were underaged. Do you think they switched up their game and started taking legal-aged girls in an attempt to avoid suspicion?"

"I've been thinking a lot about that. There's a possibility that they learned from previous mistakes and adapted to make their operation as invisible as possible. They must've figured out that juveniles were too risky and changed their MO."

"That's really disgusting. These people have no souls, treating people like chickens going to slaughter," I said.

Kerri agreed. "They should rot in hell for what they've done, but we're not in charge of that jury. All we can do is what we can do legally. I swear I'm going to do everything I can to ram the rod of justice so far up their ass is it tickles their tonsils."

I giggled. This was the first time I'd heard Kerri say anything remotely crude, and I loved it. "You're a savage, aren't you?"

Kerri laughed. "Girl, you have no idea. Somethings you have to keep under wraps."

I respected that answer. Reminded me a famous quote a history teacher had kept on his wall: Walk softly and carry a big stick. I think a president said it or something but to me, it always meant, don't make a lot of noise and you've got the element of surprise on your enemies. My interpretation could be totally wrong, but it resonated with me.

I fell silent for a moment, musing over our speculation. A thought came to me. "What if each auction had a theme?"

Kerri looked at me sharply. "What do you mean?"

"Well, at first I thought that the auction was only for girls who were virgins, but then I thought about the sheer logistics of that given this day and age and how difficult it is to find adult virgins and I wondered if maybe they tailored their auctions to kink-based themes to keep things exciting and new. Maybe they didn't stop chasing after juveniles, they just changed the theme."

The wheels were turning in Kerri's mind. "That's a pretty sharp theory. It makes a lot of sense. When we go back through the photos, we'll see if there are any similarities between the girls. Anything we can do to establish a pattern."

I smiled, feeling good about contributing something useful.

We pulled into the small parking lot designated for visitors and walked into the station. Much like the town, the police department was something out of a movie where the actual crime didn't happen, and the police officers were more like armed security guards.

I could see how Kerri knew she could break some rules coming here that she couldn't get away within the city.

Also, no offense, but I could see why Trina's

murder was never solved if the cops operating the station were any indication of the investigative power of the department.

Stereotypes were created for a reason, and the Esterdell police department fit every type.

The police chief, a round man with a bushy handlebar beard, seemed to know Kerri and enveloped her in a big hug that she clearly endured for the sake of our purpose.

"Look at you, the big city detective coming to visit," he said, his bristly cheeks plump and reddened from either too much time in the sun or rampant alcohol abuse. "Little Kerri Pope...all grown up. Imagine that. What brings you around here?"

"Actually, I was hoping I could borrow one of your computers so I can show my shadow here how we do a missing person's search." She turned to me, introducing us. "Chief Carleton, this is my job shadow, Wendy Johnson. Wendy wants to be a cop someday."

"Does she now? Excellent, excellent," the chief said, bobbing his head in approval, but there was a question in his gaze as he added, "But why come all the way to Esterdell? You can't mean to tell me that the computers at your station aren't working?"

Kerri laughed, lying through her teeth. "No,

we're under construction right now. Total upgrade for the station. No civilians allowed. I didn't want to turn her away, so I thought I might be able to call in a favor from my dad's best friend."

I tried to hide my surprise, covering with the fake, plastic smile that seemed to work on most adults and held my breath.

"You know I can't refuse a request from you," the chief said, "but shame on you for not visiting sooner. Miss seeing you around, kiddo."

"I know, just super busy. I barely even get up here to open up the house much anymore."

"Sure, sure, I understand. Big city problems keeping you from coming home. We don't have that kind of crime here in Esterdell, and we like it that way."

Except for the crimes against humanity that happened just up the road at the auction house, I wanted to murmur but kept to myself. *Oh, and the murder of Kerri's little sister. Can't forget that one.*

"It's definitely quieter," Kerri murmured in agreement. She switched subjects, saying, "And why haven't you retired yet? Surely there's an RV park somewhere calling your name?"

"Haven't found a replacement yet. Someone's gotta keep this place running smooth. Besides, what am I going to do with retirement asides from get fat and lazy? Naw, I like it right where I'm at — keeping the people I love safe and sound."

I ducked my gaze before I started giggling. By the looks of his gut, he already had the "fat" part down, but hey, kudos to him for believing he wasn't already pushing maximum density.

"So, can we borrow a computer?" Kerri asked, winking at the chief.

"You know I can't say no to you," the chief said. "Just mind the confidential stuff, for legal reasons."

"Of course. Thank you, Larry."

The chief smiled at me. "Have fun, kiddo. Most police work is all about the research. It's not all cops and robbers. Listen to Kerri, she knows her stuff."

I smiled and watched as the chief ambled back to his office, disappearing behind a closed door. He was probably going to eat a donut and take a nap.

"Your dad was best friends with the police chief?" I murmured as we settled into a private cubicle with a computer terminal. "You never mentioned that before."

"Yeah, Larry has been the law around here since I can remember. He and my dad were real close. If it weren't for Larry intervening a lot of times, I probably would've had a rap sheet a mile long. He considers me to be his greatest success story. I'm not sure I have the heart to tell him that he wasn't the reason I got my life back together. No sense in crushing the man's ego. Besides, he's harmless, and he won't think twice about anything I'm doing here."

"You're kinda taking advantage of an old man," I teased, impressed. "But you get points for being a badass."

"I'm the furthest thing from a badass, but I'll take the compliment," Kerri replied, pulling the file from her backpack. "Okay, let's get started. I can scan the photos, and then we can run a quick search."

We had a good stack of photos, but the scanning didn't take as long as I thought it would. Once the pictures were finished, Kerri made quick work of starting the search.

"Now, we wait and hope for a catch," she said.

"Is it hard for you to see your dad's best friend?" I asked.

She nodded. "My dad and Larry used to go fishing together at least a few times a month. Seeing him reminds me of my dad and how we'd drifted apart in the last years before he died."

"How'd he die?"

"Lung cancer."

"That sucks. What about your mom?"

"Also cancer, but a different kind. I guess it doesn't really matter because either one was deadly."

"I'm sorry."

Kerri accepted my condolences, lost in her own memories for a minute. I didn't have a mom that I cared enough about to mourn if anything happened to her. I didn't really have anyone.

Except for Dylan.

I'd thought I had Lora, but this experience made me realize that relationship hadn't been real either. Lora wasn't the kind of girl who was a 'ride or die' kind of friend. She was more of a 'mall or galleria' kind of friend, and I certainly had no use for that shallow of a friendship.

Crazy how it took almost dying to realize what was truly important and real in your life.

Ding.

We both straightened at the sound.

Kerri grinned with excitement as she said the words I'd hoped to hear, "Holy shit...we've got a match."

18

Goosebumps erupted along my skin as I stared. "Who is it?" I asked.

The match, a girl who disappeared when she was sixteen, had long red hair and freckles dancing across the bridge of her nose. Bright, cornflower blue eyes stared back from the missing person's database, matching with the picture of her from Franklin's stash, blood trickling from her busted lip, fear in her gaze, her shoulders bowed as she huddled away from the photographer.

Franklin had beaten her. She was most certainly dead because no one had found her in the two years since she'd been reported missing.

"Summer Godfrey, 16, was reported missing by her maternal grandmother, Linda Godfrey, two winters ago in Woodlawn. The grandmother died last year of pneumonia and was her only living kin."

"So no one is looking for her," I said. "Like Tana."

"It would seem that way."

"I don't think it's a coincidence that they target girls who have no one to care if they disappear. They're actively preying on girls who are desperately searching for a better life and won't be missed if they go missing."

Kerri nodded, flipping the photo over and sticking a Post-It note with Summer's information on it. As she was writing, another *ding* caught our attention.

Another girl, seventeen, from Brooklyn, Yolanda Rodriguez, reported missing from a foster care home five years ago. Her last living kin was listed as a drug-addicted mother without a physical address.

"We have two victims who are presumed dead with photographs of their abuse taken from Franklin Dubois' loft. Can't you get a search warrant now?"

Kerri's frustration mirrored my own. "As compelling as this evidence is, it was obtained illegally. It's inadmissible in court, which is why I didn't want you stealing anything from his place."

"But if I hadn't taken the ledger and the photos

we wouldn't have the confirmation we needed to prove that The Avalon is shady as fuck."

"You should've left it behind. If we'd been able to get it with a search warrant, we could nail his ass to the wall. Our hands are tied right now."

I glared. "This is some bullshit. We have the evidence in our hands. What difference does it make how we found it? It doesn't make any of their victims any less dead. Why the hell are we doing any of this if it's all for nothing?"

"Lower your voice," Kerri said, glancing around to see if anyone was paying attention to us. "Look, I know it doesn't seem like it, but this is good news. Even if we can't run with it to the FBI just yet, it's valuable intel. Okay? I know it's frustrating. I'm frustrated, too. I want to bring them down as much as you do."

"Not possible," I disagreed.

Another *ding* interrupted us.

Within an hour, three more victims popped up. We gathered all of the information we could from the victim information logged into the system.

In total, five were positively identified through facial recognition and matched with their missing person's entry.

The victims were:

Summer Godfrey, 16, Woodlawn, reported missing two years ago by her grandmother.

Yolanda Rodriguez, 17, Brooklyn, reported missing from her foster home five years ago.

Iris Bumgartner, 18, Manhattan, reported missing last year by a teacher who became concerned when the A-student stopped coming to class.

Jessica Lopez, 17, Queens, reported missing three years ago by an older brother who has since been in prison for aggravated assault. No other kin listed.

Parish Loughty, 17, Staten Island, reported missing from a group home six years ago. No living kin listed.

* * *

Once we were sure the search was finished, and no more victims were going to hit on the database, we collected our stuff, exited out of the terminal and left the station.

The ride home was filled with heavy silence as we processed what we'd discovered.

I wanted to feel elation. We'd found five people connected to the auction who were still missing, and they were no longer nameless victims.

But there was an entire stack of photos that we couldn't identify. Girls who'd become ghosts before they'd ever become anything worth logging into the system.

It just wasn't enough.

I wiped at my eyes, angry that I was crying over something I couldn't put my finger on. Maybe it was mental exhaustion, or perhaps it was genuine sadness for the girls who had no one to mourn them.

Either way, I couldn't stop the tears from dribbling down my cheek like a river.

Kerri didn't press me. She let me cry in peace.

By the time we reached the house, I needed a shower and some alone time.

Hicks still hadn't returned. Dylan was on the back porch, thumbing through an old photo album, lost in her own thoughts.

How did this all end? The pressure of surviving when so many had not weighed on me like a two-ton concrete slab. The fact that I'd lived when so many had died had to *mean* something. I had to *give* it meaning.

I wanted to trust Kerri, but she had too much faith in the law doing what was right. How could I trust the law when there were so many corrupt motherfuckers on the wrong side, running interference to keep the assholes safe from consequence?

Kerri's voice stopped me as I headed for the bathroom to shower. "I know you think that we're going to lose, that the odds are stacked against us, but I want you to know that I won't stop until we bring them all down."

"I know you believe that and that you'll definitely try, but you're too focused on playing by the rules when no one else is. You're going to have to break the rules, Kerri. Plain and simple. If you're not willing to do that, The Avalon will win. I can promise you that."

I didn't want to argue. I wanted the solace of hot water, pelting my skin and steam rising all around me. In my worst moments, a bracing hot shower had saved my sanity more times than I wanted to count.

And I needed it right now.

But as the water ran over my body, my mind wouldn't stop.

Something kept eating at my brain.

Something Jilly had said.

Somehow they'd known exactly how many foster homes Jilly had been in, 'down to the number,' she'd said. How was that possible? In every girl we knew about, they'd been in the system in some way or another.

The thoughts in my head wouldn't allow me to

enjoy my shower. I quickly shut off the water, toweled off, dressed, and went to find Kerri.

She and Dylan were arguing about stupid shit when I interrupted them. "Jilly said something that always seemed weird, but at the time, I didn't have enough pieces to work with. She said Madame Moirai had known she was in the foster care system, down to the number of homes she'd been in, which was confidential information. I'm willing to bet that every single girl targeted was tapped into the system somewhere."

"Like the foster care system?" Dylan asked, confused. "I ain't never been in foster care. Your theory doesn't hold up."

"Hold up, are you telling me that no one ever called protective services on your dad? Ever?"

Dylan started to shut me down but suddenly stopped, thinking. "Actually, yeah, once. I totally forgot about it. Right before I bailed. I think I was nine or ten. I came to school with a few bruises, and the school nurse had some questions. She never said, but I'm guessing she made the report."

"A school nurse would be a mandatory reporter," Kerri said, frowning as she followed my bread-crumbs. She regarded me, asking, "But what about you? Were you ever put into the system?"

"Oh yeah, several times. My mom was always riding the edge of getting popped, but she always cleaned up her act long enough to skate by, or we moved. That was her MO. Either fake it or bug out before they could catch her."

"Yeah, but what about Tana?" Dylan asked. "To hear her tell it, her grandma was a friggen saint. There's no way protective services was all up in her business."

"Actually, maybe not in the traditional sense like we know it, but Tana's grandmother had dementia, and she was Tana's primary caregiver. The state would've had to get involved at some point to make sure that Tana wasn't in danger, even if it was just wellness checks."

"I'm willing to bet that every single girl was in the system at some point, for some reason, even if they weren't placed in formal care settings," I said.

"I think you might be onto something," Kerri said. "But the sheer amount of leg work it would take to comb through the records looking for a specific type of victim...it's almost time-prohibitive."

"What if they hired a computer programmer to create a program that would do the leg work for them? All they'd have to do is have access to the database and then set the perimeters within the program."

"I mean, yeah, it's possible but Jesus, that's a pretty sophisticated operation. They'd have to create a program that was undetectable from the inside as it crawled through the records in a way that didn't trip any hacking fail safes."

"And you think a bunch of perverted billionaires with sick kinks wouldn't pool their resources to make that happen? If it's worth it to them, no price would be too high," I said.

Kerri sighed heavily, rubbing her forehead. "I don't even know how I'd go about finding out if your theory is correct. I'm no computer hacker, and I sure as hell don't know any with that kind of resume. The minute I try to use department resources, my lieutenant will be on me like flies on shit."

"Ask Hicks. If it's shady, he knows someone who does it," Dylan said. "For a former cop, he sure knows a lot of bad people."

Kerri didn't dispute Dylan's statement. How could she? It was pretty reliable. "It's worth a shot," she agreed, still mulling over the dots I'd connected. "Jilly told you that they knew all of her confidential information?"

"Pretty much. They also knew confidential information about me regarding my mom."

"Such as?"

"They knew she was a drunk," I answered.

"My buyer knew about my dad," Dylan said. "He knew my dad used to beat me. Told me to call him 'Daddy' and laughed, saying, I probably missed getting whooped and that he'd do me a solid and pick up where my daddy left off."

I shuddered, muttering, "What a dirty prick."

Dylan rarely talked about the night with her buyer. All I knew was that he'd nearly killed her, but Dylan was tougher than most. I could only imagine the horror locked away in her memories. I wanted to hug her, but Dylan didn't like that kind of blatant affection unless it was on her terms. Instead, I shared a look of solidarity, telling her without words that I understood.

Silence blanketed us. A picture didn't tell the whole story, but it offered a glimpse. We survived, but others didn't. We had to give them closure.

"Hicks should be back tomorrow. I'll have him look into the database hacking possibility. In the meantime, let's get some rest. Today has been a bitch of a day. I'm going to have a glass of wine and go to bed."

Kerri rose and grabbed a bottle of wine and a glass before leaving to do exactly as she planned.

I'd never seen Kerri overwhelmed before this moment. She'd always been our champion, our surefire cheerleader that justice would win.

Now, I could sense her faith wavering as the odds became so much more daunting.

She finally saw what we'd known all along.

We weren't going to win playing by the rules.

Kerri had to be willing to play dirty, and I wasn't sure that was in her wheelhouse.

But it was in mine.

19

The following morning, Kerri got a call from her lieutenant, putting her on a case that set off alarm bells in my head.

Hicks arrived just in time for Kerri to leave. She debriefed us like she would her fellow cops, and I think it was her way of compartmentalizing what had to happen going forward.

"A city worker accidentally punctured a casket during a mandatory plot relocation, and not one but two bodies fell out. The body of a young girl was found beneath the body of the original occupant, hidden in a false bottom. I've been called in to investigate the case."

Hicks narrowed his gaze. "A false bottom? That sounds like it was made that way on purpose.

Doesn't sound like a case of an accidental double burial."

"No, it doesn't," Kerri agreed.

"Was the body embalmed?" Hicks asked.

"Either the body was embalmed, or the victim was freshly dead because the victim was pretty well-preserved."

The memory of the embalming materials down in the basement where I found Tana's body flashed in my mind. "What if she's an auction girl?" I asked. "Why else would they have embalming fluids at the auction house? I mean, what better way to hide a dead body than to stick it with a legitimate dead body?"

"Kid's got a point," Hicks admitted, giving me props, saying to Kerri, "You and I both know dead bodies have a tendency to show up sooner or later. It's pretty smart to dispose of a victim by putting them in the one place no one would think to look — in a fucking cemetery."

"They'd have to have a mortuary working for them and the coroner," Kerri said, thinking out loud. "Which, we can probably safely assume the coroner who recently died was working for them, but what about a mortuary? There are hundreds in the city. There's no way I could get search warrants for every mortuary that ever did business within the boroughs."

Hicks shook his head. "I don't think you'd need to. All we need is one. Lawson and Bergstein handled Nova Kasey's burial, and we know Nova was an auction girl. If we can find a few more with that mortuary listed as the responsible party for the deceased, we've got probable cause for a search warrant."

"I want to go with you," I said, eager to be part of the action, but Kerri shut me down.

"It's too dangerous. You're safer here where no one knows about this place. Hicks will look out for you while I'm gone."

"I don't need a babysitter," I said, bent out of shape that she wasn't willing to bring me along when it was my idea that got the wheels turning. "And how do you know we're safer here?"

"Because there aren't any cameras, and no one knows about you here."

"We were nearly killed in a house not far from here," Dylan reminded Kerri in a cool tone. "This town isn't as safe as you want to believe it is. I mean, there aren't any cameras, but this place isn't the Garden of Eden."

Kerri glared in frustration. "You want to leave

and go back to the city? You think it's better where fucking Dubois is literally hunting you like a wild animal? Come on, stop acting like a petulant toddler, and listen to what you're saying."

Kerri was probably right, but I didn't like being left behind, and Dylan was already going stir-crazy. We weren't cut out for self-isolation even if it was the safer option. I knew the minute we were back in the city, Dylan would take off with Badger, and I would spend more time looking over my shoulder and jumping at every shadow, but that didn't stop me from blurting out stupid shit.

Obviously, we had self-destructive tendencies from our dysfunctional childhood, *duh*.

But I could sense Kerri's rising frustration, and I dialed it back because no matter how her mothering annoyed me, she was truly on our side. "Fine. We'll stay here, but you'd better come back with something useful," I sniped.

Hicks chuckled at my balls, but they should both know by now that my mouth was my own worst enemy, even with people I cared about.

"Did you find a forensic accountant who could look at the ledger?" she asked Hicks before grabbing her bag and heading for the door.

"No, but I have a feeling no one wanted to get

involved. The minute I mentioned The Avalon, doors closed. Apparently, their reputation precedes them, and they don't fuck around."

"Yeah, as evidenced by the body count of their own people," Dylan quipped. "Seems to me working for Madame Moirai is an eventual death sentence. At least Badger doesn't knock off his staff unless they've done something to earn a trip to the pit."

"Please don't start singing the praises of Badger," I said, rubbing my forehead. "So what are we going to do about the ledger? It's no good to us if we can't identify anyone but Franklin, and even that is hard to prove. He could just deny it."

"Let's focus on one problem at a time," Kerri said. "Hicks, do you have someone in your contacts who's good with computers?"

"I know a guy," Hicks answered without giving more detail.

"Good. The girls will fill you in on what I found and share our current theory. In the meantime, I will chase down this case with the extra body and get back to you."

Hicks reached out to her, catching her arm with a firm, "Be careful out there. Chances are they know we're snooping around now. The Avalon is going to have everyone on deck looking for the ledger, and

Dubois has a personal reason to get those pictures back."

Kerri nodded. For a heartbeat, it seemed they shared a private moment, but it was gone in a blink, and Kerri was out the door.

"You guys should just bone and get it over with," Dylan muttered, dropping onto the sofa with annoyance. "You're like two kids who won't admit they've got a crush, but it's obvious to everyone else."

"Mind your business, Dr. Phil," Hicks retorted, going to the kitchen to find something to eat. He grabbed a bag of potato chips and a soda before levering himself into a kitchen chair. "Tell me about the identified victims," he said, ripping open the bag.

We spent the next hour sharing everything we knew so far and our theory of how Madame Moirai was getting the intel on her targets.

"So, how exactly would someone get that kind of information without using some kind of program to comb the database?"

Hicks wiped his hands on his jeans before stroking the stubble on his chin. "Unless they had someone really high up the chain opening back door channels, a hacker could get into the database, create a secret entry point and get in and out without tripping the anti-hacker firewalls. It's a lot of work, though. They'd have to have someone on the payroll for that specific job."

"If that were the case, I would imagine that position would be worth a shit ton of money, right? They'd have to pay through the nose for that kind of service, and it's not exactly something that you could advertise on a headhunter site."

"Yeah, that's dark web shit," he agreed.

"So is your contact a dark web kinda guy?" I asked.

Hicks nodded. "One of the best."

"Are you sure it's not him that's involved?" I countered alarmed.

"You never can tell with Cy. He keeps his shit close to the vest, which is why he's the best, and no one can ever pin him down."

"How do you know him?" Dylan asked.

"I just do."

As usual, Hicks wasn't going to give up his sources. I respected that about Hicks, but it didn't help my distaste for mysteries.

Time seemed to tick by in agonizingly slow motion until finally, Kerri returned, looking exhausted after a full day in the city. I felt terrible for pouncing on her the minute she came through the door, but I needed to know what she'd discovered.

Dylan was deceptively calm as she spooned ice cream into her mouth, but I knew she was eager to hear about the body, too. She was better at hiding her true feelings than me.

Kerri hung her coat on the hall tree and walked into the living room, where she sat with a heavy groan on the sofa. "Jesus, what a long day."

"What'd you find out?" Hicks asked as I held my breath, hoping for something that would break this case wide open. "Anything worth the trip?"

"Yeah, actually, I did. What a fucking shitshow, though. Everyone's pointing fingers at who's at fault for busting up the casket and creating a hazmat situation. There are so many agencies involved. It's a clusterfuck of interagency pissing contests."

I waited impatiently for her to get to the good stuff.

"Yeah, I can imagine," Hicks commiserated.

"So, we have an ID on the victim, and she's one of the girls we identified in Dubois' stack of trophies: Parish Loughty."

I sucked in a wild breath, almost giddy at the break, even though I felt guilty for feeling anything other than sadness for a dead girl. "Parish went missing six years ago from a group home," I recalled.

"So how the hell did she end up double-stacked in a coffin with someone else?"

"That's the question, isn't it? One that I plan to ask Lawson and Bergstein tomorrow."

"It's obvious, those crooked fuckers have been covering up The Avalon's dirty work for years, but they're not going to just admit it," Dylan said, disgusted. "I say we get Badger to pay a visit to the owners and break a few bones until they confess their sins."

"As satisfying as that might be, torture is rarely a reliable method of obtaining a truthful confession. With enough pain, you can get someone to admit to killing Jimmy Hoffa when the man died before most people nowadays were even alive."

"Who's Jimmy Hoffa?" Dylan asked, confused.

"My point exactly," Kerri returned dryly. "So, no, we're not bringing in a sadist to go fuck them up for the sake of a confession we can't use."

"Fine, let's just fuck them up for the sheer joy of it," I suggested. "The only thing these people understand is pain and suffering, so I say we serve it up to them."

Dylan fist-bumped me with approval.

Kerri wasn't in the mood. "No. I'm talking to the

owners tomorrow. We'll see what they have to say about their business with The Avalon."

Dylan rolled her eyes. "Good luck on your futile mission. They ain't gonna say shit."

"We'll see." Kerri rose and told everyone goodnight. I wanted to ask more questions, but she was dead on her feet. I'd have to wait until tomorrow.

I gestured to Dylan to follow my lead, and we headed to our own bedroom.

As we undressed and climbed into bed, Dylan asked, "You think she has a snowball's chance in hell of getting them to talk?"

I sighed. "Nope."

"Me, either." A beat passed before she asked, "Should I call Badger?"

I chewed on the possibility. Badger wouldn't hesitate to break fingers and toes if we told him they were connected to Nova's death, even if only peripherally.

Regina had ended up dead after a session with Badger.

All I had to do was say the word, and Dylan would sic Badger on them.

But I wanted to give Kerri the chance to prove me wrong. "Maybe," I finally answered, "but not yet. Let's see what Kerri can do first. If she can get them to give up Madame Moirai, then great. If not, we'll send in the mad dog."

Dylan yawned. "Sounds good to me."

Within seconds she was asleep, but sleep didn't find me.

Was Parish Loughty the key to breaking The Avalon? Or was she, sadly, another dead end in a long line of disappointments?

I prayed this was the break we needed. My sanity was holding on by a thread.

I couldn't take much more.

20

When Kerri realized I wasn't going to stay behind and twiddle my thumbs like yesterday, she gave in, but only if Dylan promised to stay away from Badger while we were back in the city.

Dylan agreed, but I half-expected her to dip out as soon as we were gone.

Badger was Dylan's kryptonite. He was a poison that she couldn't stop sipping. At first, I thought it was her way of remaining connected to Nova, but now, I saw it for what it'd always been: a toxic relationship.

But there was no talking to Dylan about Badger. She bristled anytime anyone tried, including me. I didn't have the mental bandwidth to spare for Dylan's twisted addiction, so I let it go most days.

Plus, if I were honest, I knew Badger was still useful, and I didn't want to burn that bridge until we were certain we didn't need a pit bull on our side.

Maybe that made me a user, no better than The Avalon for using us, but at least in my case, I didn't leave a trail of bodies when I was through.

Hicks must've sensed Dylan was going to bail because he volunteered to keep her in check, which erupted into an argument between them.

"You're not my fucking dad, Hicks," Dylan growled. "Stop trying to boss me around. I'll go and do what I want, got it?"

"And that's how you're going to get your dumb ass killed. Be smart for once in your life and lay low," Hicks said.

"Life advice from the drunk, *oh goody*. What's next? Motivational cards on how to screw up your life and end up a loser?"

"If I do, maybe we can collaborate since you're the picture of success."

"*Ohhhh, day-um!*" I exclaimed with suppressed laughter at that epic burn. Dylan cast a nasty look my way for not backing her up, but I didn't really want her messing around with Badger unless we needed him for a specific purpose. Other than that, he was trouble we didn't need.

"Shut the fuck up, Nicole, like you're any better," Dylan shot back.

"You two bicker like an incestuous married couple," I said, untouched by her sharp retort. "It's disturbing."

"You're gross. He's like, *old*."

Among other things.

I wrinkled my nose and pushed that thought as far away as humanly possible.

"I *am* old and sick of your childish bullshit," Hicks growled. "Grow up, kid."

"Go drown yourself in booze," Dylan said, sticking her tongue out.

Hicks gestured. "I rest my case."

Kerri leveled an annoyed gaze their way. "Are you finished? We've got work to do. Get your head on straight, both of you."

I was going with Kerri to the mortuary. Dylan was going with Hicks to meet up with his computer guy at some WiFi cafe. We figured no one at the mortuary would know who I was, but as a precaution, I'd wear my wig and hoodie.

We packed up and headed out. Once we were in the city, Hicks and Dylan branched off, and we did the same.

The executive offices of Lawson and Bergstein

were located in a posh business tower in Manhattan. We were ushered into a conference room where a polished and professional secretary offered us bottled water while we waited.

We both declined. I didn't trust them not to try and drug us. I wouldn't touch anything they offered. Polite courtesy was often the gateway to finding yourself tied up like a Christmas turkey and thrown into the back of an awaiting van.

As my Gran would say, "I was born at night, but not last night!"

Two men entered the room, both good-looking in a soft, wealthy sort of way. Their tailored suits — one gray, the other navy blue — were impeccable and their personal grooming sharp.

Kerri flashed her credentials before starting. "Gentlemen, I appreciate your time. I have some questions regarding the recent discovery of a second body hidden inside a false bottom coffin that was prepared by your mortuary."

The men shared a look, then swiveled their gaze to me, saying, "Due to the sensitive nature of the situation, may we ask that your young friend wait in the waiting room?"

"Sorry, she's job shadowing me. She goes where I go today. Don't worry, she's older than she looks and currently in the police academy. Now, back on topic. About that coffin mishap...want to share with me how that might've happened?"

Neither man looked pleased with Kerri's refusal to send me out, but they didn't press the issue either. Gray Suit Guy took the lead. "I assure you, we are just as mortified as you to discover our services have been associated with such a blunder. Lawson and Bergstein has a stellar reputation going back generations, and this is a blemish on an otherwise pristine history."

"That was a lot of pretty words, but it still doesn't explain how it happened."

"We don't know how it happened," Navy Blue Suit answered stiffly. "We're looking into it."

"That's not good enough," Kerri said. "Here's the thing...that second body, the female? She was a 17-year-old girl reported missing from a group home out of Staten Island six years ago. So that missing person's case has just been elevated to homicide because, as you can imagine, there's no natural way that girl's body ended up in your coffin by accident."

They both looked appropriately appalled. "That's horrible," Gray Suit Guy murmured, and his partner agreed. "I assure you, we have no idea how she ended up in one of our caskets."

"Do you sell many double-decker coffins in your line of work?" Kerri asked.

"There's no market for 'double-decker' coffins as you put it, and even if there were, it's not something we would typically offer."

"But, two bodies spilled out of one of your coffins that were discovered to have a false bottom. I'm sure you can see how that looks from my end."

"And how pray tell, does it look?" Gray Suit Guy asked with a deceptively mild tone. "Because I'm not sure I'm following where you're going with this in terms of Lawson and Bergstein."

"Let me spell it out for you: a murder's been committed, and a coffin prepared by your company was used to hide the evidence of that crime. The only way that could've happened is if that coffin was prepared especially for that purpose, which again leads us straight to Lawson and Bergstein. It makes me wonder...what would happen if we called for an accounting of everybody Lawson and Bergstein prepared for burial?"

"You and I both know that's absurd," Navy Suit Guy retorted, but his gaze shifted to his partner.

"Is it? Not from where I'm sitting."

Gray Suit Guy steepled his fingers and narrowed his gaze. "We want to be helpful, but I sense we are spinning our wheels together. We didn't have anything to do with that poor girl being interred with another body, and we plan to do a thorough investigation into how it happened. Unless you're here to charge Lawson and Bergstein with a crime, I'm afraid there's not much more we can say without the presence of our lawyer. We offer our sincere condolences for the family of the young lady but—"

"We know Lawson and Bergstein is owned by Avalon Inc.," I blurted out, unable to keep my mouth shut. "I doubt it's a coincidence that a girl identified as the victim of a human trafficking network was found buried by a mortuary owned by the company associated with that same network. So, I guess the biggest question is...how do you sleep at night knowing what you're a part of such a disgusting operation?"

I could feel Kerri vibrating with anger that I'd spilled the beans, but I couldn't take their bureaucratic bullshit another minute longer. They were playing games just like Dylan said they would. They felt smugly safe with The Avalon's protection, and I wanted to shake them up.

"I don't know what you're talking about, and those are some wild accusations, young lady. Surely, they're teaching young cadets how the law works."

"I know how rich assholes work, and that's all I see in front of me right now."

"I think we're done here," Gray Suit Guy said, rising. "Pleasure speaking with you. If we discover anything of value, we'll be sure to call Lieutenant Stilman."

Kerri stilled, and I nearly crowed at his sloppy mistake. How did he know to speak to the one person who kept throwing Kerri off The Avalon's trail? The air in the room changed as Kerri rose with a cold smile, saying, "You may think you're in a position of power because who is backing you, but I can assure you...you're in as much danger as anyone who's signed a deal with Madame Moirai. Let me tell you something, gentlemen...she's cleaning house. Many of her former associates are dead. Think about that. How secure do you feel in your role that you don't fear ending up the same way? Maybe it wasn't your fault, but all eyes are on Lawson and Bergstein right now, and something tells me that's not going to make the queen bee very happy."

Both men looked uneasy. Kerri slid her business card across the table. "If you feel like talking, we can offer you protection. If not, best of luck. The Avalon is going down. Are you going to go down with it?"

As soon as we were clear of the building, Kerri unleashed on me.

"What the fuck were you doing, Nicole? You could've blown everything. You don't show your Ace before you're ready to go for the kill. You just threw all our cards on the table, and it could've backfired."

"But it didn't. You were brilliant," I gushed, too excited by Kerri's show of steel to be hurt by her anger. "You put them on blast, and it showed. I think they pissed their expensive suits."

"Look, I get that you're balls-to-the-wall willing to do whatever it takes to take down Madame Moirai, but that's reckless and dangerous behavior. That's how people make mistakes and get killed. If you can't keep your mouth shut, you can't come with me anymore."

I realized she was serious. I might've really screwed the pooch in there. It was sheer luck and Kerri's quick thinking that saved the situation. "Fuck, I'm sorry," I said, my giddy excitement fading. "I just saw them dancing around your questions, acting so superior, and something snapped. I want to see them pay for what they've done, and I want them to be afraid of what's coming. It won't happen again," I promised, but I wasn't sure that was enough. Kerri was really pissed and questioning her judgment to let me tag along.

"It's really frustrating when you and Dylan go behind me and unravel all the threads I've tied together when we're supposed to be on the same team. Saving your damn asses is fucking exhausting."

Anyone else would've bailed on us by now. Kerri was doing her best, and we had to stop making it harder for her. I reached out with genuine remorse. "I swear I won't open my mouth. I'll let you handle things, but please, don't leave me behind. Being part of the solution helps me to feel less helpless. In a small way, it feels like I'm taking back some of the control I lost. I guess that's weird but—"

"It's not weird," she assured me, blowing out a heavy breath, "but I can't have you running your mouth like that. Not ever again. There's an art to interrogating people. It's not like in the movies when the cop just hammers at the suspect, demanding answers. It's a dance. A subtle weaving of a web that gets tighter and tighter until the suspect has nowhere to go but where you want them to. There was nothing subtle about what you did back there. We're just lucky it went our way."

I nodded, feeling like a jackass. I had a lot to learn about police work. I peeped at her, repeating with awe, "You were really impressive. Like, as in badass. Until this moment, I might've underestimated you."

Kerri snorted derisively. "You don't say? Well, glad I finally passed the test. I've only put my entire career on the line to save your ass, but I'm so relieved you finally believe I can do the job."

I smiled at her sarcasm. "Now you sound like Dylan."

She chuckled despite her lingering irritation. "Yeah, I guess I do. I'll have to work on that."

Speaking of. "Do you think Dylan and Hicks have killed each other yet?"

"Probably. Let's hope they get what they were looking for before they start to tear each other to pieces."

21

Before reconnecting with Hicks and Dylan, Kerri got an angry call from her lieutenant, demanding that she turn her ass around and get back to the station. We didn't have time to stash me someplace, so I had no choice but to tag along. I couldn't play the part of the job shadower around her colleagues, so we agreed upon a variation of that lie if anyone asked.

As far as the station was concerned, I was in a mentorship program for at-risk youth, and Kerri was my mentor.

It didn't need to hold up to intense scrutiny, it just had to make enough sense to keep people from wanting to dig a little deeper, and I was getting pretty good at selling the lie.

But our quick prep work was all for nothing. Her

superior didn't even look twice at me when we walked in. His eyes were burning two holes straight into Kerri as he called her into his office and slammed the door behind them.

The blinds immediately jerked shut, and the shouting started.

What was the point of a door if he was going to scream loud enough to startle the heavens? Aside from a few curious glances, no one cared that Kerri was getting her ass reamed behind that flimsy door, but no one noticed my presence either, so apathy seemed to be contagious in this place.

"Who the fuck told you to go harassing Lawson and Bergstein? I just got an angry fucking call from one of our best and most loyal civil servants saying that you practically accused them of murder over some girl who was probably a drug-addicted hooker? C'mon, Pope, what the hell are you doing here? I hesitated to put you on this case because you've got an unhealthy fixation with open and shut cases—"

"There's no possible way that girl ended up in that casket organically," Kerri interrupted her voice strong and without a waver. "The casket had a false bottom, and that girl was put inside to hide the evidence of her murder. If you can't— or won't — see that, the bigger question is why."

She'd thrown the gauntlet without coming out and straight-up accusing the motherfucker of being a corrupt son-of-a-bitch on the take, which we all suspected he was but couldn't prove.

At least not yet.

"You're barking up the wrong tree, Pope," the lieutenant growled.

"Am I?" she challenged. "Because the way I see it, I'm on the scent, and it's leading me straight to where you don't want me to go. Why is that, lieutenant?"

"You're walking on dangerous ground. Watch it."

But Kerri was on a roll, and she wasn't backing down. "There are dead girls all over this city, and I've got proof that there's a sophisticated human trafficking network operating behind the scenes. The question is...how deep does the corruption go?"

"You're out of your mind with delusions of grandeur. Seriously, you think you're going to crack some mega case and make a name for yourself? Well, get in line, girl. Every detective dreams of getting that one case that catapults them to the top of the heap, and this ain't it. You're wasting your time and the department's time chasing ghosts."

"I disagree."

"Well, luckily for you, it ain't your fucking call."

"If you pull me from this case, I'll go over your head," she said, that thread of steel returning to her voice. "This case is bigger than whatever petty bullshit you've got going on against me."

"Don't flatter yourself, Pope," the lieutenant returned sourly. "Ever ask yourself why you've never been promoted to lead detective in spite of the years you've got on Cudgel and Blaine?"

"The fact that you're a fucking misogynist who secretly hates strong women?" Kerri answered.

"Get the fuck out of my office with that feminist bullshit agenda. No, that's not why. It's because you're too emotional. You can't separate your personal feelings from the job. It's the reason you can't let go of that drunk ex-partner of yours, Hicks. You don't know how to put things in the right boxes and that always drags you down. At least Hicks has the brains to know his limitations. You, on the other hand, are dumb as fuck. Now get the fuck out of my face. I don't want to hear more shit about you harassing Lawson and Bergstein over some harebrained theory about dead hookers. Unless you've got something more solid than your opinion, drop it. You hear me?"

"Loud and clear."

"Good."

Kerri emerged from her lieutenant's office. I expected to see hot rage burning in her eyes, but something far more intense radiated from her pores — cold, hard resolve.

"Are you okay?" I murmured as we hustled from the building. "You look like you're about to cut a bitch."

"That fucker just pushed me over the line. I always knew he was a stupid piece of shit, but now, it's obvious I can add corrupt as fuck to his resume, too."

I agreed. "I don't understand how he can look at the evidence and turn the other way. It's like, right there in front of him."

"Stilman has a taste for expensive things. My guess is that The Avalon sweetened the deal with enough cash to make it worth his while to turn a blind eye."

"Or maybe he enjoys the perks of having access to something he shouldn't want," I suggested quietly. "Cops can be pedophiles, too."

Kerri nodded discomfited. "Yeah, I know. It's a weird thing to hope that someone is only ethically corrupt and not morally, too. I mean, Stilman can suck a dick for all I care, but I hate knowing that someone who took the same oath as me, could be so fucking wrong in the head."

"So, what are you going to do? It sounded like he threatened to fire you if you kept chasing this case."

"Fuck him. I'm not going to stop. I'll go over his head. I hadn't wanted to bring in the FBI, but maybe it's time to explore that option."

"I thought you said you didn't know if we could trust the FBI?"

"I don't, but I sure as hell know that we can't do this on our own, especially if Stilman is blatantly running interference. I have a contact in the Bureau I can talk to, feel it out. Until then, I'll keep doing what I've been doing — my fucking job. If Stilman wants to try and fire me over this, he'll have my union rep so far up his ass he won't know where she starts, and he begins. Either way, it'll buy us time to get this shit done."

This was the version of Kerri I needed on our side. Sure, I liked the kind and caring version, which brought us food and made sure we weren't devolving into degenerates, but let's get real, that Kerri wasn't going to save our asses.

I'm sure Dylan would agree — this Kerri kicked ass.

And fuck that guy for dragging Kerri down for

having a heart on the job. Maybe Hicks was a lost cause in most people's eyes, but compassion was a dying trait, and we weren't better off for its loss.

Seriously, maybe if people had more compassion for other people, I wouldn't have felt the need to sell myself for the chance at a better life. Maybe other auction girls wouldn't have died to satisfy someone else's itch.

Societal break-downs were measured by more than economic benchmarks. People had to care about other people, or else the framework of human connection failed.

Every single auction girl had needed someone to care about their welfare, and yet, society had utterly failed them.

Tears stung my eyes. My heart hurt for the loss of fragile Tana and quirky Jilly, two people who changed my life and were gone because society was fucked.

"Are you okay?" Kerri asked, noticing my sudden quiet and the shine in my eyes. "I need you to be strong. The storm's about to get real bad, real quick."

I wiped at my eyes. "I'm fine. What's our next step?"

Not satisfied, but knowing we didn't have time for a heart-to-heart therapy session, Kerri moved on.

"We need to find Hicks and Dylan and then get back out of the city. Now that we've shaken up Lawson and Bergstein, no doubt they placed another call to their Avalon contact, and we just became Public Enemy Number One. There's probably a price on my head along with yours."

Made sense. Madame Moirai's solution to unfortunate situations seemed to be murder. Who was this fucking evil bitch, and how did she get away with so much carnage? "So, back to the country?"

"For now. I don't feel comfortable staying in the city for too long."

I accepted her plan even though I wasn't thrilled to return to the sticks. There was a certain level of peace in not continually looking over my shoulder, but the absolute stillness only encouraged my brain to fill the void with memories I couldn't stomach revisiting.

However, dodging a mental break-down was preferable to being dead, so that put things in perspective real quick.

We met up with Hicks and Dylan in Central Park as they wolfed down dirty water dogs from a street vendor. At least they hadn't killed each other, that was worth celebrating.

Hicks said, "Cy knows a guy who runs a website

on the dark web who might be interested in running this story if we can't get some traction from the bigger news outlets."

"Press?" Kerri asked, unsure. "How's that going to help us?"

"Look, I don't like the press either, but we need eyes and public pressure. We can't get that on our own. We need to shine a spotlight on these motherfuckers so they can't scurry back to their dark corners and wait out the scrutiny. We need people who aren't afraid to throw names in the fire, and Cy might know a guy who fits that criteria."

"Cy is your hacker friend?" I asked.

"Friend is a generous term, work associate is more appropriate," Hicks corrected around a hot bite. "But yeah, his handle is Cyb3r Plague and he's known for pulling Anonymous-level hacks on shitty people. The best part is, the minute I mentioned Franklin Dubois, he knew exactly who I was talking about. It seems he's got a bit of a grudge against the man, and he's more than willing to make his life a living hell for personal reasons."

"Well, hot damn, that's awesome," I said, pleased. "By all means, let's loop him into Operation: Avalon Assassination."

Dylan snickered. "I like it. Can we get shirts made?"

"When it's all over, and we win...hell yeah," I joked.

"Don't order the ice cream cake just yet," Hicks warned. "Just because Cy has a personal stake in taking down Dubois doesn't mean he's interested in tangling with The Avalon. He's heard of the network, and he said they don't fuck around. They've got a serious body count, and no one can seem to drag them down because they're well-insulated from any attack."

"Good feelings gone," I murmured. "Why can't we get a fucking break? Just once? Okay, so maybe Dylan's plan to let Badger fuck with Dubois is the better option. He's a soft prick. He'll break easily."

"Sounds like the most efficient plan, in my opinion," Dylan quipped, finishing her dog. "Besides, payback should be satisfyingly bloody and *bone-break-y*, don't you think?"

I laughed at her savagery, shrugging in agreement. "It is satisfying."

Kerri threw up her hands with a shake of her head. "Stop talking. You're incriminating yourselves, and I don't want to know the shit you've done with Badger. *Jesus*."

Hicks chuckled because nothing seemed to rattle him. Except being locked in a country house without a bottle of Jack. "Let's hit the road," he said. "But we're making a stop at my place first."

I had three guesses what he wanted to pick up, and the first two didn't count. Oh well, we all had our coping mechanisms, right?

Seemed Kerri didn't want to add that fight to our battle and simply accepted his request.

Hey, at least Hicks wasn't an angry drunk.

One thing life had taught me — take your victories where you found them.

22

After a few days in the country, Hicks got a text from Cy that didn't sit well with any of us.

"What's it say?" Kerri asked.

Hicks frowned as he read. "He's got something for us, but he wants me to bring Nicole when he delivers."

Kerri's expression screwed into a ferocious scowl. "Fuck that. Why does he want to meet Nicole? That doesn't feel fishy to you?"

Hicks' dark expression told us he didn't like it either. "I don't know why he wants to meet with Nicole, but he said he wouldn't turn over the information until he talks to her first."

"This feels like a fucking trap," Kerri said,

shaking her head. "The answer is no. She's not going."

"Hold up, we need the information. He said he's got what it takes to bring down the whole organization. It might be worth taking the risk."

"To who? I'm not willing to serve Nicole up on a plate for whatever he's promising to deliver. What the fuck is wrong with you that you would even consider this, Hicks?"

"Calm down, I never said we should do it without taking precautions," Hicks barked with a glower. "Something's in play, and we know it. We go in expecting that it's a trap and account for whatever they're planning."

"Except we don't fucking know what Cy is planning or if he's compromised," Kerri said. "Look, I don't care how you spin this, I'm not sending in a kid to do an adult's job. No negotiating. I won't budge on that score."

Everything Kerri said rang true. It definitely felt like a trap with the supposed information as bait, but what if Cy was truthful and he needed to tell me something personally? *Yeah, I know, long shot, but desperation was a significant motivator.* We could spend the rest of our fucking lives tip-toeing around the shoreline, but we'd also never catch the big wave that way.

"I'll do it," I announced, shocking both Kerri and Hicks but not Dylan.

Dylan and I understood the risks and knew everything we did was a gamble, whether Hicks and Kerri wanted to admit it or not.

"Like hell you are," Kerri disagreed. "All my instincts tell me this is a trap. I'm not sending you into a dangerous situation. I don't care what kind of information Cy is supposedly dangling in front of our faces. Your life isn't worth losing. We'll find another way."

"What if this is the only way? We're not dealing with amateurs. Madame Moirai is a killer, and she's good at what she does. If Hicks' hacker guy has found something and the only thing he's asking is for me to show up to get it, I think that's an acceptable risk."

"I don't." Kerri's stony expression was set in cement. She wasn't going to budge.

I suddenly understood what that shit-bag lieutenant of hers was saying about Kerri. Unlike her fellow cops, she did put her heart above her head. The smart play would be to send me in to get whatever leverage we could manage because this was a game of extremes. We would either win, or we would die.

All of our lives were on the line. We didn't have the luxury of picking and choosing which chance we could take. Sometimes opportunity didn't knock politely, it whispered from a dark alley.

"I'm doing it," I told Kerri firmly, but before she could protest, I added, "and you're going to keep me safe. Think of me as bait. You've done this before, I'm sure. It's not like you're sending me in there without protection, right? I'm not worried. We'll get what we need, and we'll get out."

"What if things go wrong?" Kerri asked.

"They won't."

Her sad smile was knowing as she said, "Things always go wrong. Nothing ever goes as planned. I can't put you in that kind of danger. We'll find another way."

Dylan piped in. "So, we'll all go. It'll be a goddamn Brady Bunch picnic. Let this fucker try and mess with all of us. We'll eat him for lunch."

I smiled with affection at Dylan. I knew she'd walk into fire with me if that's what it took. Her courage gave me strength."See? We got this," I assured Kerri. "How dangerous could one computer nerd be?"

It was meant as a joke, but Kerri was wound too tight to appreciate the humor. Death lurked in every corner, every shadow, but we couldn't change that unless we took risks. I was done hiding.

If this computer nerd wanted to chat me up in exchange for the information we needed, I'd be his Chatty Cathy. If he thought I would be an easy target, I'd show him that I'd go down swinging.

Kerri must've sensed she wasn't going to sway me. Frustrated, she said, "I need a minute," and walked outside to get some clarity.

Hicks pursed his lips, shaking his head, but he remained quiet. He knew the stakes just as we did. He also knew this was our best option, but he wasn't going to push. Kerri would come to the same realization on her own, even if she hated it. "She's got a big heart," he said with a hint of regret. "She can't help herself. It's one of her best qualities...and one of the worst for the job."

"That's what Stilman said," I said with a snort.

"Fuck him. He doesn't get the privilege of passing judgment on her."

Yeah, agreed. Fuck him and his corrupt soul.

Even if he would never say in so many words, I saw the genuine affection Hicks had for Kerri. I wished things were different for them, but even if we weren't fresh out of miracles, we definitely didn't have any to spare for these ill-fated soulmates.

It was crushingly sad to watch, but there wasn't anything I could do about it.

Hicks rose slowly from his chair, sighing as he said, "I'm going to see if she's all right" and left us alone.

The steady tick of the clock on the wall was the only sound in the room.

I met Dylan's gaze. A small, resigned smile twisted her lips. "We could all end up dead, you know."

"Or we could get our hands on the jackpot," I countered, desperately needing to believe this could work out for us.

"Pretty high stakes."

"The highest."

I dropped my stare to my lap, slowly flexing my hands when I realized how tightly clenched they were. "I just want this to be over. Don't you want this to be done?"

"That's a stupid question."

"We're chasing our tails, running from people trying to kill us, constantly worrying about every little sound and blind corner...I can't do it much longer." Dylan nodded, but there was something in her eyes that told a different story. "What's wrong?" I asked.

"You mean, aside from the obvious?" she asked.

"Yeah, aside from that."

Dylan heaved a heavy sigh, considering her answer before she said, "I want this to end, I do. It's just that I've never had anyone, aside from Nova, who made me feel like I was part of something important. Like I mattered just for being me. You make me feel like that. What happens when we're not forced to have each other's back anymore? What happens when you go off to college, and I go back to the streets?"

"Who says you have to go back to the streets?" I challenged.

"Nicole, I have a sixth-grade education. Where else do you think I'm going to go? I can't go off to school like you. No future for me doesn't include operating beneath the fringe of society. C'mon, you and I both know that."

"Bullshit," I said, shaking my head. "You're fucking smart, Dylan. You can take the GED and go to college with me. So what if you don't have much of a formal education. You've more than made up for that with your natural ability to figure shit out on your own. You've got something most people don't —

grit. And I'm not going to listen to you give up on yourself just because your path is different than most."

Dylan looked away but not before I caught the sheen in her eyes. It was a scary thing to reach for something that previously you'd been told wasn't for you. I reached for her hand, squeezing tight. "When this is all over, I'll still have your back and not because I have to, but because I want to. You're a part of me, and you always will be."

Dylan sniffed, clearing the emotion from her throat. "Yeah? Even when I'm an asshole?" she asked, half-teasing, but I saw the stark fear in her eyes that I might abandon her someday.

"You're an asshole most days, so yeah," I assured her, my voice cracking.

At that, she broke into soft laughter because there was no denying that Dylan was an acquired taste, but I couldn't imagine her any other way.

And I told her so. "You're the sister I never realized I needed, and I found you in the most fucked up of places, but I don't regret having you in my life. You've saved me as many times as I've saved you, and no one will ever understand us like we understand each other."

God, that was the honest truth. We were broken,

but the cracks weren't scary because we saw ourselves in each other, and that made us feel less alone.

Big, deep feelings were hard to navigate for people like us, and enough was said on that subject.

"You're not that hard to figure out," Dylan quipped with a watery smile. "You're the most basic bitch I know."

"I'm not basic," I disagreed.

"Totally basic," she shot back with a slow grin. "But I love that about you."

We laughed together, enjoying the simple pleasure of the moment before it faded then I drew a deep breath and said, "Let's take down these motherfuckers once and for all."

Dylan held my gaze for a long moment then slowly nodded. "Yeah, let's do this," she said, adding wistfully, "Maybe college won't be so bad after all. I've always kinda liked the idea of learning more about animals and shit."

"What kind of animals?"

"I dunno, all of them, I guess. I had a dog once. I always wanted to get another when I was older and could protect it, but that hasn't happened so far. The timing never seemed right."

I didn't need details to know that her dad

must've killed her dog. If the man weren't already dead, I'd want to kill him myself.

"I say the first thing we do when this is over, is you get a dog," I declared.

"Yeah?"

"Hell yeah. I like dogs. Why not?"

The light in her eyes brightened at the prospect. "Okay, I'm getting a fucking dog."

"Dylan, the vet? I can get on board with that. It has a nice ring."

Dylan's shy smile was everything. That was what hope looked like, and it looked good on her.

Now, all we had to do was survive.

Same shit, different day, but hopefully, we were at the end of that *Ground Hogs Day* rerun because we were all ready for a new ending.

And holy fuck, we deserved it.

23

We left for Cy's place, armed to the teeth with concealed weaponry. Hicks and Kerri were carrying their sidearms, along with a few surprises hidden in their boots while me and Dylan had blades.

If this was a trap set by The Avalon, they weren't going to get us without a bloody fight.

In the past, Cy had always met with Hicks in secluded places with good Internet connections, like the WiFi cafe but not today.

This was the first time Cy had ever given Hicks his actual address, another sticking point that gave Kerri hives, but we were committed, and we were doing it, come hell or high water.

Cy lived in a ratty, rent-controlled building in an industrial area. The sound of water dripping behind the walls told a story of black mold and rats scurrying from view as we climbed the steps to his apartment.

I was pretty sure if we left with our lives, we'd still leave with Hep C.

Hicks and Kerri looked hard as nails, eyes sharp as they watched every corner, tensing at every sound. We reached the door, and Hicks knocked with Kerri beside him, their bodies shielding us from view.

The whine of an electronic swivel grabbed our attention, and we looked up to find a surveillance camera perched in the corner, giving the occupant full view of who was at the door. Smart for a guy who probably regularly pissed important people off. People who had the resources to hire a hitman at that.

The door buzzed open, and Hicks walked in first. The apartment was unlike anything I'd ever seen. Computers of every size and shape covered every surface. A sophisticated surveillance system was running on four different monitors. Cy had seen us coming all the way from the street level.

An older man, a little pudgy around the middle, wearing thick glasses and a flannel shirt with jeans rose to greet us, his nervous energy reminding me of a crack addict trying to act normal when in fact, he was high as fuck.

"Hey, hey, nice to meet you." Cy extended his hand straight toward me, and I stared at his outstretched hand like it was covered in dog shit. He took the hint and withdrew his hand. "Right, so, this is weird, huh? Why'd I ask you to come here when I could've just given the intel to our friend, Hicks. Well, I, uh, had to meet the girl responsible for doing what no one else could. You're kinda like a celebrity in certain circles."

"What the fuck are you talking about?" I asked, sharing an uncertain look with Kerri and Dylan. "Who's talking about me?"

"Well, I mean, you know, people in my circles. The dark websters."

Dark websters? Blech, this guy was trying too hard. "Why would anyone on the dark web be talking about me?"

"Because you've been making waves for a bunch of people who pay a lot of money to keep their waters calm for smooth sailing."

"Cut the crap, I don't care who's talking about her, do you have the information we need or not? This game you're playing isn't amusing," Kerri growled.

"Ahh, of course, and you must be the sharp, underestimated detective out to prove something to the world, Kerri Pope. Otherwise known as Adrian Hicks' better half on the job."

"Do you have what we need or not?" Hicks asked, his tone as annoyed as Kerri's.

"Don't I always deliver?" Cy returned with a smug grin. "Yes, I have what you're looking for, but first, I want to talk about how you did it. I've been trying to get dirt on that fuck, Franklin Dubois, for years, but the man is squeaky clean in cyberspace. He doesn't even watch porn. Who doesn't enjoy a little adult entertainment now and then? Am I right? So, color me surprised when Hicks came to me with the ledger...it was like the Holy Grail of dirty secrets."

"I thought you said you were taking the ledger to a forensic accountant?" Kerri muttered beneath her breath at Hicks.

Cy came to Hicks' defense, "Don't bust his balls too bad. I know it's hard to believe, but I have a degree in accounting. Kinda goes hand-in-hand with illegal computer hacking. Gotta love numbers and codes, but only one actually pays the bills."

Dylan, disinterested in the man's jabber, started to wander around the apartment, ignoring Cy's stern, "Hey, don't touch that" as she poked and peeked at whatever caught her eye.

Cy returned to me. "So, spill the beans...how'd you catch him?"

"I figured out the code on his secret safe. He kept everything in there. I grabbed it and ran."

"So simple yet eloquent in execution," Cy said, his gaze darting back to Dylan before returning to us. "I should've known he was an old-fashioned paper guy."

"How do you know Franklin Dubois?" I asked.

"Let's just say back in the day when I was a greedy capitalist, he was the attorney for the man who stole my company's idea to revolutionize the programming used for billable hours. I know it seems small, but his client ripped off my coding and walked away with twenty million dollars when he sold the program to the largest corporate billing company in the business. It's made me a little bitter, to be honest. After that, I made it my goal to take down every single person who was involved with the theft of my intellectual property."

"Did it work?" I asked, curious.

"Did what work?"

"Your plan for vengeance."

"Mostly, but Dubois was the slippery fish. Until now."

O-kay, cool story, bro. "Can we get what we came for, please?"

"Sure, it's right over here," he said, gesturing for us to follow. The apartment had big windows facing another building, typical for New York, but I didn't like how the building opposite us seemed empty.

Kerri and Hicks seemed to read my mind. The tension in the air thickened. Hicks said, "Why are you stalling?" and pulled his gun. "Did you rat us out, Cy? How much did they offer you for Nicole?"

"Whoa! Hold up, what's happening? We're just talking, right? Like friends do. Chatting it up. Sharing war stories."

"We aren't friends, and you're never this chatty. What the fuck is going on, Cy?"

Hicks advanced toward him, and Cy glanced behind him out the window, almost as if pleading for someone to take care of the problem, which sent my heart racing. Kerri was right, this was a fucking trap.

I turned to tell Dylan we were leaving when the unmistakable sound of a bullet puncturing glass liquefied my guts and sent me straight to the floor. I covered my head as more bullets started to rain into the apartment.

"Stop, stop! I did what you asked!" Cy cried out, diving to avoid the hail of bullets seeking any target.

This was a free-for-all. They planned to make sure no one left that apartment alive. If Cy was stupid enough to make a deal with The Avalon, he deserved to die like the traitor he was, but I didn't want to die with him.

Hicks yelled to us, "Stay low, get to the door!" while he and Kerri took defensive positions behind the shelter of the wall space between the windows. They popped out long enough to shoot in the direction of the gunfire, but it was a blind shot with little hope of connecting with the shooter.

I started to make a move toward the door, but I realized Dylan was army crawling her way toward Cy, her knife in hand. "Dylan, no!" I cried out, but she was determined to get what we came for, and if that meant gutting the computer guy to get it, so be it.

"We're not leaving without what he promised," she said, launching herself at Cy and tackling him to the ground while Kerri and Hicks traded shots with the shooter, buying us time.

Dylan wrapped her legs around his torso and her arm wound around his neck, the knife at his throat. "Give us what you promised, asshole, or I'll end you right now."

The threat was genuine. Even though Cy

outweighed Dylan by a hundred pounds, she had the strength of a street kid used to fighting people bigger and stronger than her. She pressed the tip of her knife against his throat when he tried to throw her off him. "Don't make me slit you from ear to ear," she said. "Give us what we came for!"

"I can't! They'll kill me!"

"I'll kill you, motherfucker," Dylan said against his ear. "And there won't be enough left of you to bury when I'm through, computer man."

I scrambled toward Dylan, hoping to appeal to Cy's sense of self-preservation. "If she doesn't kill you, I will. Be smart and give us what we came for. If what you said is true, we can take down The Avalon, and they won't be able to threaten you or anyone else, but if you play their game, you're dead anyway. The Avalon has been killing every single person they deemed a security leak. What the hell do you think you're going to be considered if you walk out of this apartment?"

Dylan tightened her grip around his neck, pressing the tip of her blade a little deeper into his skin. He sucked in a pained breath, wheezing with fear when he realized Dylan would filet him like a fish.

"The zip drive on my desk!" Cy gasped. "*Jesus-*

fucking-Christ, it's on my desk! I swear it! Don't kill me!"

I ran to grab the drive, shoving it in my pocket, but not before Kerri yelled, "I'm out!" and kicked over a table for cover.

Hicks paused to reload, but the front door burst open as two assassins ran in, pausing only long enough to shoot Cy in the head, splattering Dylan with brain matter, the traveling bullet narrowly missing her face as she pushed Cy away.

Hicks exchanged gunfire with the second gunman, taking him down with a shot to the head, but I heard rather than saw Hicks take a hit as he went down.

"Hicks!" Kerri shrieked, the sound chilling my blood. There was too much happening at once to process the sheer carnage in that room.

I rolled away, ducking behind the sofa but not before seeing Dylan get stuck beneath Cy's inert body as the assassin took aim. I screamed, panic, and fear driving me forward as I pitched myself at the man and shoved my knife deep into his throat.

I didn't see the shot, but I saw Dylan fall to the floor, and I lost it.

"Nooooo!" I half-crawled, half ran to drop to

where Dylan lay slumped, her sightless eyes staring up at the ceiling as blood poured from her chest.

I tried to stop the bleeding. It was too much like Jilly. I hauled her into my arms, crying and babbling at once. "No, no, you're not allowed to leave me like this, Dylan. Noooooooo!" I pressed against the gushing wound as her lifeblood emptied from her body, and I held her tight, losing all sense of reason. "She needs a hospital! Call an ambulance! No!" I slapped at hands, trying to grab at me. My tears blinded my vision. "Call a fucking ambulance!"

"She's gone, Nicole!" It was Kerri, and she was yanking at me. "We have to go, now!"

"No," I wailed, unable to leave. I couldn't leave her along with that sad sack of shit, his brains plastered all over his stupid computers. She deserved better than to be left behind in this shit hole! But Kerri wasn't taking no for an answer and hauled me to my feet with a strength I didn't know she had.

"Move it!" she yelled in my face, and it was then I realized tears were streaming down her cheeks, too. I couldn't make sense of what had happened, but there were dead bodies everywhere.

Shattered glass, blood, and burnt electrical.

"What the fuck!" I screamed at no one in particular, maybe God, in total shock. Kerri, ignoring my protests, dragged me from that room with the force of a gorilla, throwing me into the car before peeling away from the scene of our ultimate heartbreak.

They were gone.

Dylan and Hicks, both gone.

Oh my God, oh my fucking God...in the blink of an eye, everything had changed.

What the fuck were we going to do now?

24

From that point forward, everything was a blur. We were covered in blood, shaking from shock and crushed by grief. All of our places in the city had been compromised. We had no place to go except one.

And it was the last place I wanted to be.

Badger opened the door, and his eyes widened when he saw the state we were in. He didn't joke or say anything shitty, somehow he knew.

I confirmed it when I said dully, "Hicks and Dylan are dead," and then I collapsed against him, blood and all. I sobbed until I couldn't produce sound or moisture; my throat ragged and screaming for water or booze.

Kerri sat on the sofa, her gaze as ragged as my

soul. She said nothing as I told Badger how everything had gone down.

Badger handed both of us bottled water and listened.

I drank greedily before continuing. "It was a trap. He was supposed to get us there, and then the sniper in the building across the street was supposed to take us out. When that didn't work, they sent two more assassins to finish the job. Hicks took out one but not before taking a bullet. I took out the other, but not before he got to Dylan. I couldn't move fast enough. Everything was moving in slow motion. I tried Badger. I tried to get to her." My voice cracked, and I had to stop before the tears started again. "And we had to leave them behind. Oh my God, Badger, we had to leave them behind!"

Badger sat in silence, digesting the news. When he finally spoke, he seemed harder, more vicious than I'd ever seen him. "You were going there for something...did you get it?"

I wiped at my eyes, nodding. I pulled the zip drive from my jean pocket with shaking fingers. "I don't know what's on it, but Cy said it had everything we needed to take down The Avalon."

Kerri roused imperceptibly, unaware that I'd gotten the drive because I hadn't had time to tell her.

She didn't seem to have the strength to deal with that right now. Tears welled up in her eyes as she rose stiffly. "May I use your shower?" she asked in a hoarse voice.

"Yeah, sure," Badger said, bouncing the drive in his palm, as Kerri disappeared into the bathroom. "So, what's on this?"

"I don't fucking know. I don't even know if Cy was lying to save his own ass. I don't have a computer capable of reading the drive."

"It's nothing special. A simple laptop should be able to open it," he said, grabbing his own. He fired up the computer and pushed the drive into the port. A folder popped up on the screen. "Let's see what was worth dying over," he murmured as he double-clicked.

A massive file with docs, photos, and financial records opened, and all I could do was stare. "I don't understand, why had Cy put this together if he was just serving us up to The Avalon?" I asked, confused.

"He probably started with good intentions, then realized what a fucking goldmine he was sitting on and figured he could cash in with two paydays. One, serving you up to The Avalon and second, using the info for blackmail purposes later. It's a good chip to have in your pocket. It's what I would've done."

"Fuck you, Dylan is dead for this," I whispered, my heart cracking in two. "What am I going to do with this information now?"

"Let's take a deeper look at some of these docs." He double-clicked a file. I sucked in a wild breath. Holy shit...names, addresses and phone numbers, known associates, aliases, anything that could be attached to someone's confidential file were included for each person. "It's the key we needed to decipher the ledger. Holy fuck, he did it. We can put names to nicknames now."

He double-clicked a photo. I gasped and averted my gaze as soon as I saw what it was. Murder porn. Each image was labeled with the name of the auction girl and her buyer.

Tears dribbled down my cheek. This was the motherlode. This was what The Avalon had been so desperate to keep from surfacing.

But Badger seemed focused on one thing. He scrolled to find Nova's name. I held my breath. He clicked on her file.

His eyes glazed over at the photos, but I felt the rage building inside him, burning away the last of his humanity as he forced himself to read everything about her buyer. He vibrated with dangerous energy, but he moved to the next file, Dylan's.

I couldn't look.

However, Badger was a man on a mission. He created a separate document of names and addresses, but before he could print it out, I added two more names. I knew why he'd made a list, and I approved.

He was going to kill Dylan and Nova's buyers. I met his gaze. I wanted to kill Tana and Jilly's. "I'm going with you." Badger didn't question, just nodded. With a single shared look, we had a silent pact to end those who had brutalized our loved ones.

As a failsafe, he made a copy of the drive, finishing right before Kerri emerged from the bathroom. I told him in private, "Just you and I. Kerri doesn't need to know."

Again, he accepted my terms. Kerri couldn't deal with what I had to do. She'd just lost the man who, in another life, might've been her soulmate. I'd lost my soul sister. We all had ways of grieving.

Mine involved exacting vengeance.

Kerri, somewhat revived by the shower, returned to us with a somber but clear headspace, asking what we'd discovered on the drive.

We told her.

A single tear escaped before she wiped it away. "Good. They died for something. I have a contact with the FBI. I'm going to turn it all over."

I nodded, agreeing it was probably the best route, sharing a secret look with Badger that Kerri, thankfully, missed.

We spent the night combing through the drive, learning how Madame Moirai built her network, how she funded it and kept it moving undetected for ten years.

How she used the list to further her career and rise to her current position.

There were two lists: Decommissioned and Elevated.

Decommissioned was just a fancy word for dead, and elevated was life-long sexual slavery.

Not sure which was worse.

Eventually, they all ended up decommissioned anyway.

The list of corrupt individuals part of the network was mind-blowing from doctors to lawyers, royalty to billionaires.

And I was right — there were auction girls selected according to theme or kink.

She had to keep the buyers interested in the next best thing.

The youngest auction girl had only been thirteen.

Lawson and Bergstein Mortuary embalmed the

decommissioned girls. They then packaged them into the false bottom of a casket scheduled for a civilian burial. The family of the deceased, never knowing that a murdered girl was lying beneath their loved one.

But the biggest reveal was one that knocked the air out of my lungs.

"That bitch," I murmured, staring at the identity of the notorious Madame Moirai — Head of Social Services, the seemingly kind and gentle Bitsy Aldridge.

And to think she'd actually saved me from Franklin that night. Irony at its best.

Had she known who I was? That I was the one trying to destroy everything she'd built? I guess I'd never know.

We snatched a few hours of sleep, and then the following morning, after we'd confirmed who wasn't on the take with The Avalon higher up the chain, Kerri took the drive and went to the Bureau to turn over the evidence to the Human Trafficking Task Force.

I stayed behind and waited for the all-clear.

She called two hours later. "It's done. Arrest warrants are being processed as we speak. Lay low for the time being."

I hung up and looked to Badger. We had a short window to make this happen — a week, tops.

Kerri picked me up, and I made plans to meet up with Badger later that night when everyone was asleep.

Killing was best done under cover of night.

There were going to be five men who wouldn't make it to trial. Trials took too long to satisfy the rage in my heart. I needed swift and lethal judgment in payment for their debt.

I looked forward to their screams.

One in particular...

"I'm coming for you, Franklin. It's your turn to bleed."

EPILOGUE

News of The Avalon, the biggest underground human trafficking network, broke on all the news outlets as the FBI chased down every single person associated with the auction.

It was the most sweeping bust of all time. Careers were ruined and made, a few Avalon associates took their own lives rather than suffer through the public scrutiny of their crimes and some were outright murdered.

If Kerri knew I was involved with five deaths associated with The Avalon, she never said anything and I didn't volunteer.

After some discussion, I moved in with Kerri and agreed to get my GED, although it felt a little pointless after everything I'd been through. Still, I needed something to do with my time and studying seemed a good alternative to the therapy I desperately needed at some point.

The Avalon assets were frozen by the FBI as the investigation began in earnest. I had an attorney representing my interests and I was assured that as soon as those assets were freed, I would be first in line for a settlement but money didn't replace the people we'd lost.

The only solace I took from the promise of a settlement was the knowledge that I'd been adamant about the creation of a victim's fund for the families of the lost girls.

But I wanted a special settlement set aside in Tana, Jilly and Dylan's names.

I wanted to make sure that Tana's grandmother had the best care before her dementia took over completely. I wanted a scholarship for veterinarian science set up in Dylan's name for a kid with Dylan's background.

As for Jilly, we discovered, she had a little sister, Jade. I wanted the money to go to her because that's what Jilly would've wanted.

We recovered Dylan and Hicks' bodies and mourned them properly but we were never able to recover Jilly's body, which hurt my heart everyday.

Kerri had the pleasure of putting her own lieutenant in handcuffs for being on the list and running interference for The Avalon on the inside. The FBI offered Kerri a job on the task force but she declined, saying, she'd had enough of seeing kids battered and bruised for a lifetime. Instead, she accepted the lieutenant position that had recently opened up.

Even though I no longer had to watch over my shoulder or wear a wig to go to the corner bodega, something felt unsettled. I couldn't put my finger on the cause until five weeks later, an envelope arrived, addressed to me.

I opened the envelope to discover a handwritten letter from Olivia.

Dear Nicole,

I knew you would be the one to tear it all down. I envied your strength and hated myself for my weakness.

But I'm so grateful.

The night the auction house went up in flames, I was sent to placate the man known to us as Henri Benoit, later identified as Franklin Dubois.

I heard he was murdered in his bed. I will never shed a tear for his death. He was the wickedest of men and terrifying.

Which is why I'd been pressuring you so hard to

elevate. It was an act of self-preservation. Madame Moirai had threatened that if I couldn't get you to accept his offer, I would take your place.

I was willing to do or say anything to get away from him. I knew I would die at his hands.

When I realized that the house had burned down, I knew it was my only chance at freedom.

During the chaos, me and the masseuse, Jenny, ran away together.

I know I don't have the right to ask but I hope for your forgiveness someday.

We were all victims but you were the bravest of us all.

Forever grateful,
Dana (Olivia)

I CLOSED MY EYES. I always swore I would never find charity in my heart for that woman but today felt different. I touched the tiny cross necklace at my throat and I smiled as tears filled my eyes.

A circle had closed.

That unsettled feeling faded like mist in sunshine.

Moving on felt possible for the first time in weeks.

Tana, Jilly and Dylan would forever live in my heart as the bravest, most incredible women ever born.

They would always remain a part of me.

Warmed by the knowledge that no matter where I landed in this life, I would never be alone, filled me with purpose and humbled me with grace.

My spirit was guarded by bad-ass guardian angels and you couldn't ask for better than that.

ABOUT THE AUTHOR

J.H. Leigh is a pseudonym of USA TODAY best-selling author Alexx Andria. She enjoys writing about angsty, emotional stories with deep personal impact. You can find her on social media for more information about her books.

"Books are magic."

ALSO BY J.H LEIGH

THE GIRLS THEY STOLE

THE GIRLS THEY LOST

THE GIRLS THEY FEAR

Made in the USA
Monee, IL
19 February 2021